BOOK 3 IN THE
*Kemmons Brothers
Baseball Series*

Heal MY HEART

ELLEY ARDEN

author of *Save My Soul* and *Change My Mind*

CRIMSON
ROMANCE

F+W Media, Inc.

Published by
Crimson Romance
an imprint of F+W Media, Inc.
10151 Carver Road, Suite 200
Blue Ash, OH 45242. U.S.A.
www.crimsonromance.com

ISBN 10: 1-4405-7496-0
ISBN 13: 978-1-4405-7496-2
eISBN 10: 1-4405-7497-9
eISBN 13: 978-1-4405-7497-9

*To my parents, who never blinked when I wanted to play hockey,
football, and soccer—with the boys. Thank you for celebrating me
for who I am, not who you wanted me to be.*

Acknowledgments

Women's professional full-tackle football exists—and there is no lingerie involved. These amazing women are strong and determined to play a sport they love at a level that challenges them. But they need fan support to keep their leagues up and running. I urge you to check out The Women's Football Alliance (*http://www.wfa-football.net*) or the Independent Women's Football League (*http://www.iwflsports.com/*) to find a team near you.

As always, I'm eternally grateful for the insider's perspective my husband, a team physician, and his colleagues provide me with. Pro athletes are impressive, but the men and women who keep them on the field are extra-special.

This book closes out the Kemmons Brothers Baseball Series, so I'd like to acknowledge Jennifer Lawler, who gave the first book in this series—and me—a chance. I've been blessed with wonderful editors along the way, but none more influential than Tara Gelsomino, who worked with me on this final book. Thank you.

Chapter One

Beer did not belong at baseball games. Not on a Sunday afternoon when there were little, jersey-wearing kids in search of foul balls, not foul mouths.

M. J. Rooney rolled her eyes in commiseration at the clearly uncomfortable kid sitting on her left while the loudmouth behind them spewed vulgarities at the first-base umpire, who was no more than forty feet away. How had the kid's dad not said anything yet? He sat on the other side of the boy, drinking his beer like the antics of the man behind them were perfectly tolerable.

They weren't.

The jerk stood for the millionth time today, bumping the back of M. J.'s head with his knee.

She growled and faced her friend and roommate, Tanya, who was seemingly as oblivious to the commotion as the kid's dad. "You know? If I wanted to deal with drunken fools, I could've picked up an extra shift at the bar—and gotten paid for it."

Tanya's face wrinkled while she chewed a mouthful of popcorn, and then she shrugged her broad shoulders. "Aw, come on. This is fun."

Not for M. J. The rude person behind her aside, she struggled with being a spectator and would much rather be out on the field, even if baseball wasn't her game. Sitting in a stadium filled with thousands of screaming fans summoned a tsunami of adrenaline, making her muscles twitch. She was pretty damn sure she could throw that ball more accurately than Cleveland's last two pitchers. After all, accuracy was the hallmark of any quarterback worth his or her weight in eye-black.

"Fans, please stand for the seventh-inning stretch," boomed a voice over the loud speaker.

M. J. stood if for no other reason than to give her muscles some action.

"Is that a Clash jersey?" The Neanderthal behind them snickered as he poked a finger into Tanya's left shoulder blade. "That's a Clash jersey." He stuck out his yellow tongue. "Girls can't play football. That's a joke."

Right before Tanya turned around, she flashed M. J. "the look"—the one that said, "Bitch, you're dead," when directed at the opposing team's cornerback, who was heading straight for M. J. outside the pocket.

"You got a problem with women playing football?" Tanya asked, getting way up in the guy's face, which wasn't hard with her six-foot-one frame.

A few people around them stared, while others obliviously swayed as they sang "Take Me Out to the Ball Game." Right about now, M. J. would've given anything to have someone take her out *of* the ball game, because if the tightening in her gut was any indication, this wasn't going to end well.

"*I* play football," Tanya spit. "You wanna make something of it?"

The guy's glossy eyes widened, and M. J. gripped Tanya's wrist in a show of peace as much as solidarity. Where M. J. would do her best to diffuse the situation with words, Tanya, the daughter of a boxing coach, preferred to use fists.

"Ooh. Is that your girlfriend?" The guy howled at his own juvenile question.

The guy next to him tried distraction with the least-effective action—he handed him another beer. Just what the jerk needed, more alcohol.

M. J. reached for Tanya's other hand and tugged on it to turn her around. The singing stopped. People around them returned to their seats, but M. J. refused to sit until Tanya sat, too. All the while, she wished her best friend and captain of the O-line didn't feel the need to represent the team *everywhere* they went. Pride was an excellent thing, but unfortunately, this wasn't the first time Tanya's apparel got them into trouble outside the Clash stadium. People just weren't that open minded when it came to women playing football.

One of these days, the Clash was going to win a championship and, along with it, some respect. Then maybe they wouldn't become targets for assholes who couldn't run a mile, let alone suit up and compete with a women's professional full-tackle football team.

Back in their seats, M. J. noticed the staccato rise and fall of Tanya's chest as she tried to calm herself down. "He's not worth it," M. J. said. "If you get into another fight, Coach will bench you." Tanya's dark eyes locked on M. J. "I need you on the field."

"Fine," Tanya snapped, nostrils flaring.

They turned their attention back to the game. M. J. focused on the pitcher, trying not to let the run-in with the guy behind them spoil her only day off this week. An inning later, the boy beside her stood to let his father pass.

"You sure you don't want to come, bud?" the man asked from his place in the aisle.

The boy shook his head and wiggled a mitt onto his left hand. "No way. Polla hits a lot of fouls."

M. J. smiled. She liked kids. One of her favorite parts of being a professional athlete was signing autographs for boys who were shocked she could actually play, and girls who suddenly realized they had every right to play, too.

Five minutes after the boy's father left, the unmistakable crack of wood meeting leather ripped through the stadium, bringing everyone on the first-base line to their feet. The ball hung in the cloud-splotched sky.

The kid reached his glove overhead, hitting M. J. in the jaw. She didn't mind, though. In fact, she'd locked onto that ball like a pass-starved wide receiver. If she had anything to do with it, *this* kid was getting *that* ball.

And he did.

The bullet hit her left shoulder before it tumbled into his glove. She winced, but shook it off. At least it wasn't her throwing arm. And the kid … he was beaming … until the jerk behind them reached for the ball, jostling the glove.

"Lemme see it!" He sprayed beer-tinged spit into the air.

Horror flashed on the child's face as the ball rolled out of his glove, hitting the seat, only to be scooped up by the drunken man.

"Finders keepers," the guy said, laughing.

"Give it back," the boy shouted. "It's mine."

People around them agreed, but the man pretended to spit-shine the ball on his T-shirt and shook his head.

Tanya growled. "Give the ball to the kid."

All M. J. could see was Tanya's fist connecting with the guy's fleshy cheek—which was warranted, but not the way M. J. wanted to start this football season—so she shoved between the confrontational pair as best she could and attempted diplomacy. "Come on. He's been waiting all game for one. He's just a kid." She held her hand palm up. "Be the bigger man."

The guy laughed. "I think your girlfriend's the bigger man."

Tanya lunged, and M. J. steeled against her. As the man wobbled in his drunken state, M. J. grabbed the ball. She had just enough time to pass it off to the child before the guy's two-hundred-fifty-plus frame careened over their seats, falling into M. J., who felt the railing scrape the back of her thighs.

"Grab my hand," Tanya yelled. But it was too late.

Bottom of the eighth, M. J. Rooney face-planted on the right field warning track.

• • •

Dr. Tag Howard kicked his feet onto the seat of the chair across from him and admired the image on the phone being shoved under his nose by the team's orthopedic surgeon, Dr. Marcus Kent. As far as game coverage went, working with Marc was optimal, because it meant Tag gave up his complimentary seats in the stadium so Marc's wife and three kids could see the game instead. That way, Tag could stay in the clubhouse.

It wasn't that Tag didn't like watching baseball—or any other sport for that matter. He just liked fixing hurt athletes better. Besides, being near the field reminded him of not-so-pleasant things.

"She's gorgeous," he said, eyeing the platinum paint job on the Mercedes S-Class that Marc was considering buying.

"Look at this interior." Marc swiped a finger over the screen, changing the picture.

Tag held the phone closer. He could almost smell the flawless, hand-stitched leather. The image of top-of-the-line perfection warmed him somehow. Maybe it was time for him to get a new car. Maybe this one, if Marc wasn't buying it.

"What's holding you back?" Tag asked.

Marc chuckled. "The $95,000 price tag. Meredith's off to college next year, and that's a semester and a half of tuition payments."

Tag nodded even though he didn't have a clue as to what college cost these days. He'd been lucky enough to be adopted by a wealthy family who paid his tuition in full—all the way through med school. A charmed life, he'd been told. And it was, if he didn't think about what came before Edna Dean and Simon Howard opened their Shaker Heights home to an unwanted nine-year-old boy.

"So lease it," Tag said, chasing away the memory with the power of his voice and passing the phone back to Marc. As he did, the silver box lit up and vibrated.

As team physicians, their phones went off all the time, but Tag thought he recognized the name of the texter—and it was the last name on earth he expected to see.

Squeezing his eyes shut, Tag reset his brain. It couldn't be his biological brother's name flashing on Marc's phone. Tag must've been seeing things, a vision brought on by his earlier thoughts.

It's not him. Calm down.

But no amount of rational thinking could stop his throat from squeezing shut. He turned his head toward the television to hide his discomfort, and cold sweat covered his skin. He tried to swallow hard enough to break the blockage and get some air to his lungs so he could stop the panic, but he failed.

"Huh. Jordon Kemmons has a player he wants you to see," Marc said. "He asked for your number."

Bad joke, Tag thought. But it couldn't be a joke. As far as he could tell, no one outside his adoptive family knew about his biological connection to baseball's storied Kemmons brothers.

"How 'bout I tell him I'll pass his number along to you?"

Tag nodded. Somehow the motion loosed the knot in his throat, and he reminded himself that Jordon wanted to talk about a player, not rehash their abysmal childhoods that ended up with awkward Tag in a foster home while his athletic brothers, Jordon and Grey, were placed on the fast-track to professional baseball.

Marc's palm landed on Tag's back. "You have arrived, my friend. When the biggest agent in baseball comes a-callin', you're the real deal. Do you think it's Causeway? I heard he's struggling with rehab after the Tommy John surgery. If you get Causeway back on the field, every agent in baseball will be referring players to you. Damn! How'd you get so lucky?"

"I have no idea," Tag whispered.

The minute he accepted this job with the group of physicians who covered Cleveland's major athletic teams, he worried the day would come when his past collided with his present. But he wanted this, worked hard for this—the opportunity to prove to his biological father wrong. There was a place in professional baseball for a boy like Tag, just not on the field, where Tag had received the brunt of his father's emotional abuse.

Now, it was time to face the consequences of that decision.

Tag's stomach churned, but he banished the unrest with a deep inhale. He'd keep a barrier between himself and Jordon. His office manager could call Jordon's assistant and arrange for the injured player to be flown to Cleveland for a consultation. It happened all the time. Agents went outside team medical sources for second opinions. Sometimes they accompanied the player, sometimes they didn't. Under the circumstances and with a mutual history riddled with discomfort, Tag figured Jordon would want to stay as far away as he could.

"Is that a fan on the field?"

Tag snapped his head in the direction of the television suspended on the far wall. The first baseman, Johnnie Foreman, and an umpire were bent over a lump on the warning track.

Marc was already out of his seat. "This night just got a whole lot more interesting."

After Jordon's text message, it was interesting enough, as far as Tag was concerned. He had no desire to be close to the field on the heels of that, but he jogged behind Marc toward the hallway staircase that led to the dugout. No matter what the injury was, if it happened in the seats, paramedics took control, but if it happened on the field, it was the team physicians' jurisdiction. Not knowing whether the injury was orthopedic or medical meant they both had to assess the injury. Lucky him. Tag cringed.

"Probably some drunken idiot," Marc said, right before Tag took a huge breath and stepped onto the field.

Marc couldn't have been more wrong.

Just beyond first base in the dirt of the warning track, a woman stared up at Tag with watery, translucent eyes. They were the color of a Caribbean sea and, suddenly, the unrest that plagued Tag the minute he stepped onto the field waned. Whoever she was, she was gorgeous, but the blank expression on her sharply angled face bothered him.

"She just came to about a minute ago," Chris Chalmer, the team's trainer, said.

"Anything broken?" Marc asked.

If anything was, that could be Tag's cue to step back and let Mark take over. Then Tag could work his way off the field and return to the comfort of the clubhouse while Marc and Chris tended to the break.

But Tag knew it was a concussion the minute he saw her vacant stare.

He dropped to his knees.

The wind picked up around them, tossing a ribbon of caramel hair across her face where a strand stuck between her lips. She didn't move except to blink.

Hooking his finger around the loose bend of the strand at her ear, Tag tugged it free on instinct.

She smiled, and something other than discomfort at his current on-field location buzzed in his blood. He ran with it, if only to get through the exam.

"Hi, I'm Dr. Howard. What's your name?"

"Maya Jane," she answered. Her voice was soft and scratchy. "But don't call me that. I hate that name."

He nodded, holding in the smile he wanted to release. This wasn't the time or place. They had an audience—and not just the small group of players, officials, and medical staff surrounding them. Forty thousand pairs of eyes were wondering a) what happened and b) when the game would resume. The field was one big arena of judgment.

"Get the hell off the field," a fan heckled.

Those exact words were a one-way ticket back to a rundown little league field in Milwaukee, Wisconsin, where Tag had heard his biological father spout the very same thing—because there was "no place in baseball" for an uncoordinated kid like him. And apparently, there had been no room in Francis Kemmons's life for a boy like that, either.

His breathing weakened as he confronted the demons again, but as he focused on the peaceful blue of the woman's eyes, his pulse settled, too. "What's your last name?" he asked.

"Rooney."

"Then how about I call you Miss Rooney?" Tag glanced at her left hand to make sure "Mrs." wasn't more appropriate. When he didn't see a ring, he bit back another smile. This one slightly more troubling, because it was born from an undeniable attraction—something he shouldn't be thinking about during an exam.

"Fine."

"Good. Miss Rooney, how did you end up on the field?"

"It's my job to be on the field."

Tag raised his brows and looked up at Marc.

"Concussion," Marc mouthed.

Tag gave his head an almost imperceptible nod. For all he knew, Maya Jane Rooney wasn't even her name—although making up an identity would take one hell of a blow to the head.

"Do you know where we are, Miss Rooney?"

She nodded, but then she inhaled and her eyes rolled upward with a flutter and her body swayed from its sitting position.

The team trainer caught her from behind.

"Call for the cart," Tag said over his shoulder.

Laying on her back on the warning track, the woman stared up at him. "Did I get sacked?"

Sacked? Like fired? Tag shook his head. He didn't detect an accent, but maybe she was from another country where the phrase meant something different.

"You fell," he said. "We're going to get you to the hospital for some tests."

She mumbled something.

Tag leaned closer until he could feel her warm breath on his cheek and smell her spicy perfume. The normal slow jog of his heartbeat turned into a full-on sprint. "What did you say?"

"I hate hospitals," she whispered. "I hate doctors, too."

That was worth a chuckle, so he let loose.

"Then this is going to be a long night for you," he said, thankful he wasn't the emergency room doctor who'd be on the receiving end of her disoriented disdain.

She sat again, and her hand shot up to grip her neck, her pretty face crinkling.

"Does your neck hurt?"

She answered with a vacant stare.

"We're going to board her."

Ten minutes later, Miss Rooney was strapped in and hoisted onto the cart. As Tag watched her get driven away toward the exit in the left field wall, his phone buzzed. He glanced at the text from Marc. It was the contact information for Jordon along with a note:

After that circus act, I bet you're ready for some real sports medicine. Ha! Let me know what he says.

Somehow, Tag had forgotten about Jordon, and now that he was reminded and feeling uncomfortable in the middle of the baseball field, he was oddly sorry he wasn't accompanying Miss Rooney. Whether she hated doctors or not, an evening with her sounded better than an evening spent worrying about contacting his brother.

Chapter Two

M. J. laid a hand over her eyes, shielding herself from the overhead light. Her head hurt. Her stomach churned. If it were any other day, she might try to blame the discomfort on the woman standing at the foot of her bed.

"Maya Jane, your father is not pleased."

M. J. grimaced at her stepmother's chiding but didn't doubt the sentiment. Dad was rarely pleased when it came to his only daughter. Still, the woman, who'd spent the last twenty years telling M.J. she loved and supported her as much as if she'd given birth to her, could've at least waited until she was out of the hospital to launch into the lectures.

"He can barely think straight with worry," Felicia continued.

And yet, he wasn't here. He hadn't even called.

"This is the biggest case he's heard since his appointment, and the trial requires all of his attention."

Good thing his daughter never did.

"How are we doing?" The booming male voice was a nice change from Felicia's high-pitched rattle.

The short and stout emergency room physician who'd been in and out of M. J.'s room since she arrived hours ago, stood over her.

"How do you feel?" he asked.

M. J. dropped her hand to the sore side of her neck. "I've been better."

"And you will be better again. It's a mild concussion, and you just need to take it easy."

"No football," Felicia blurted.

The doctor confirmed it.

"For how long?" M. J. whispered at the doctor, trying not to think of Felicia's glee, which would become Dad's glee when he heard the news. His daughter playing professional football was a thorn in his side; he viewed it as nothing more than a teenage rebellion gone awry, an excuse for M. J. not to grow up and get a *real* job. He was wrong, but over the years she'd gotten tired of trying to explain what football meant to her.

The doctor tugged a pen from his breast pocket and clicked the top. "You're out until you're cleared. You'll need to follow up with your team doctor tomorrow in the concussion clinic. For the rest of today, take it easy. No physical activity. Limit your exposure to electronics. And if the symptoms worsen, notify your physician immediately, or go to the ER." He said that last part while he was looking at Felicia. "Watch her closely, Mom."

M. J. almost snorted. Mom? Felicia had never baked her cookies or read her bedtime stories. No one would ever mistake the woman for June Cleaver.

She did have the nagging part down though.

"Absolutely," Felicia said, eyeing M. J. up with the same you-heard-the-man look she had perfected during M. J.'s limit-testing teen years. "And no shifts at that filthy, noisy bar, either." Felicia nodded for emphasis, and then addressed the doctor. "We'll make sure she follows orders."

No doubt they'd try. Dad and Felicia had been trying to force M. J. into some neat little mold for twenty of the twenty-seven years she'd been alive. Dresses, makeup, high heels. *Couldn't you try out for cheerleading instead? Don't you want to be a ballerina like your stepmother? Stand up straight. Sit like a lady. Majoring in physiology is a waste.*

And the beat went on. *No football. No shifts at the bar.*

"Did I hear someone say something about following orders?" Tanya stood in the doorway with a bottle of Gatorade in hand. Her keys swung around the index finger of her other hand.

Felicia grimaced and looked away. There was no love lost between the pair. Being one of those women who started sentences with "I'm not a racist, but …" Felicia couldn't quite get past Tanya's skin color *and* the fact that she played professional football, too. One or the other, maybe. But both? Never.

M. J. closed her eyes again. *Damn concussion.* If she'd been in her right mind, she'd never have let Tanya call Dad in the first place. There hadn't been a voicemail M. J. had left for him over the past decade that wasn't addressed by Felicia first.

"We're just going over discharge orders," the doctor said.

Tanya laughed. "Good luck with that. A quarterback doesn't take orders; she gives them."

Felicia's dramatic sigh filled the room. "Well, she's going to listen now. Maya Jane … " her hand landed on M. J.'s ankle, "you need to come home with me where you can rest and be waited on hand and foot. Right, doctor?"

"Sounds good to me," the man said.

It sounded terrible to M. J. She hadn't lived at home since she was eighteen. She would never willingly put herself back in a place where she fell short of expectations just by breathing. "I'll be fine."

"She'll be good." Tanya stepped forward. "I got this."

Felicia sighed again. "Your father isn't going to be happy with you."

He never was, but when she'd broken every record in the league's book and powered the Cleveland Clash to a championship, he'd have to acknowledge she was at least good at it.

M. J. pushed off the elevated mattress using the aching muscles in her back. Shit. She felt like she'd been sacked by Washington D.C.'s freight train, CeCe George. Except that getting up after a hit like that was the best feeling in the world. Certainly better than dealing with disapproving family members.

The weekly injury clinic at University Hospital, where M.J. would see Dr. Ridge, couldn't come fast enough. If she had anything to say about it, she'd be cleared in time for tomorrow evening's practice.

• • •

Tag stared at his cell phone resting beside his laptop. The damn thing seemed to be alive, taunting him. He tried to focus on the MRI results on the computer screen, but his gaze kept wandering back to the phone as if it had spoken to him: *When are you going to call your brother back, chicken? Buck, buck, buck. How 'bout now?*

"How about never?" Tag spouted, and then looked at his open office door before standing up to close it.

Of course, Jordon had to go and be a dick about this by refusing to give details or make arrangements through Tammy. His message had been crystal clear and befitting of his reputation as a hardline negotiator: *I will only talk to Dr. Howard.*

But Dr. Howard didn't want to talk to him.

Dropping his elbows to the desk with enough force to hurt, he roughed his face in his hands and growled. "Fine." He'd call, because if he kept up like this much longer, he'd be certifiably crazy, and that wouldn't get him to the top of the sports medicine world.

Calling Jordon, on the other hand, might.

With a deep breath, Tag tapped through to Jordon's number, reminding himself this was business. It'd been twenty-five years since they'd said a word to each other, with no attempts at contact in between. He wasn't a sniveling nine-year-old anymore. He was a focused and determined thirty-four-year-old, who could handle a professional call without getting sentimental. From what he'd heard, Jordon wasn't the sentimental type either. There was no reason to believe this call would disintegrate into a discussion of the past.

A gruff hello interrupted the second ring.

Tag opened his mouth, but no words came out. Worse, his mind blanked.

"Hello?" Jordon said again.

"This … is Dr. Howard." Making a professional call, he told himself. *Be professional.*

"Tag." There was just enough of a pause after Jordon's voice faded to inject emotion into the silence, making Tag squirm.

He'd spent the last twenty-five years of his life trying to forget the emotionally abusive family he'd come from. He didn't want to deal with anything but an injured baseball player now.

"How are you?" Jordon asked.

"I'm well." It was a rote and inaccurate answer, considering the searing pain in Tag's chest. "What can I do for you?" He had the impossible wish that if he didn't acknowledge the connection, then Jordon wouldn't remember him.

But Jordon had been the oldest. He had to be close to forty now. Certainly, a fifteen-year-old Jordon would've remembered Francis Kemmons's drunken tirades and humiliating coaching sessions even better than a nine-year-old Tag did, which was saying something, because, after twenty-five years, Tag still heard the man's voice as though he was standing behind him.

You're too weak, boy. Weak boys don't play baseball. They grow up to be sissies.

Tag swallowed the jagged emotion pressing into the walls of his throat, and yanked the glasses from his face.

"I need you to take a look at Grey," Jordon said.

Tag squeezed his eyes shut and shook his head against the thickening silence. Unbelievable. It wasn't enough to be contacted by Jordon, but the injured player was his brother, too.

"I don't know if you heard about the injury," Jordon continued.

"I did." It had been all over the news. Even if Tag hadn't been a sports medicine doctor and team physician, even if he hadn't been related to the injured party, the sheer horror of a decorated athlete nearly sawing off his throwing hand would be astonishing news. "But I thought he was progressing."

"He is. Everything internally seems to be healing miraculously, but they have to keep stopping therapy because the wound site re-opens."

All of a sudden, the reason Jordon would single out Tag despite their troublesome connection became clear. "You heard about my research, didn't you?"

"Actually, one of the trainers mentioned it. I … sat on the information for a while not knowing if I should call."

Again with the personal innuendos. Tag winced. His eyes blurred and burned. It had to be psychosomatic. He hadn't struggled with his vision since the surgery ten years ago—unless you counted the ridiculousness of wearing reading glasses at such a young age. Still, it was better than being legally blind in one eye because of a congenital cataract that nobody in your biological family cared enough to fix. He dipped the phone away from his mouth and exhaled. Getting through this call would be so much easier if the focus remained on work.

"I might be able to control the dehiscencing by using pig bladder as a scaffold to re-grow the tissue," Tag said, hearing the sureness return to his voice.

"That's what I've been told."

"But I'd have to see him first—make sure he's a candidate."

"That's what I was hoping you'd say."

Tag rubbed a palm over his face as the bulk of his brain scrambled for a way to backtrack and get out of this meeting. The other small but noisy part of his brain chastised him for even considering turning down the opportunity to use experimental treatment to put a Gold Glove centerfielder back on the field. Something like this could put Tag on the radar of every agent and team manager in the game. It could make him an integral part of major league baseball, something Francis Kemmons said he'd never be.

"I, uh, don't know my schedule off-hand, but you can call my office. Tammy will set him up."

"Tag …" Again with the emotionally-charged pause. "Thank you."

"Don't thank me until it works."

Or at the very least, until he kept the appointment. A second after hanging up, Tag was back to thinking up ways to get out of it.

A knock at the door rattled him. "Come in," he called.

Fran poked her head into the room. "Lunch is here. You better get some before Dr. Ridge eats it all. He was drooling during set up."

"Thank you." Tag returned the nurse's smile, knowing they'd ordered his favorite brick oven pizza for the afternoon's Fellows' clinic.

Come to think of it, he did need to get out of this office—and out of his head—and he needed to give his stomach something to do other than churn with worry over seeing his brothers again.

Pizza would help.

• • •

M. J. sat on the exam table, trying not to let the nervous energy swing her feet hard enough to rattle the metal sides. If Dr. Ridge didn't clear her, she was going to freak. The Clash's season wasn't a long one. Heck, they barely had the backing for the six regular-season games they played. Missing even one game would be detrimental to her pursuit of a championship, a league-passing record, and MVP. She needed those things if she was ever going to get the kind of public accolades that would make her image-conscious father realize that, despite his judgmental tendency to declare right and wrong for everything, there was more than one way to define success.

"Dr. Ridge will be right with you. He's running a little behind."

M. J. blinked at the woman who disappeared as suddenly as she'd appeared. *Great. More waiting.*

She watched as people passed the open door to her exam room. Some looked in and smiled, but she couldn't manage to muster the strength to smile back. In fact, she was just about to get up and close the door when a handsome man in a white coat passed. They made eye contact for a brief second before he disappeared in the same direction the nurse had.

But then he was back.

"You," he said, smiling.

It was a wonderful smile, bright and white, balling his cheeks and squinting his eyes, defining his chin with a sexy v-shaped crease.

"Me?" M. J. questioned.

He stepped into the room, wearing the same smile along with a pale blue dress shirt and crisply pressed gray pants visible from the split in his white coat. "You don't remember me, do you?"

"No." One word was a better bet than letting her incredulity slip out amid a full sentence. If she'd met a man like that before, she'd certainly never forget him.

"You're Miss Rooney, aren't you? I examined you on the field after you fell."

M. J.'s jaw dropped. "Oh," she managed, despite the embarrassment heating her face. If she didn't remember him, God only knew what she'd done or said during their exchange. She wasn't exactly mealy-mouthed.

"How are you feeling?" He tilted his head and rolled his gaze over her, a hint of that smile lingering in his beautiful hazel eyes.

Physically? "Better." Mentally? Like a fool, because she was trying to place him, but nothing that happened after she toppled over the railing and before Felicia arrived at the hospital made sense. And now she was gawking at this crazy-attractive man.

"How'd you end up at Fellows' clinic?"

"Dr. Ridge." She matched the tilt of his head with her head. "He's my team physician."

Dr. Sexy's eyes widened. "Which team?"

"Clash," she said without hesitation, maybe even a little too fiercely. She'd just been laughed at too many times to count.

When he chuckled, she wanted to slap him, but he looked so damn good doing it.

"Now it makes sense," he said. "You told me you belonged on the field when I asked how you got there, and then you asked if you'd been sacked."

He wasn't laughing at the fact she played football? Interesting. On the other hand, he was laughing at something she said, which begged the question, what else had she said? Did she tell him he was hot? Probably. But if she did, she didn't want to know, unless maybe he'd told her she was hot, too. On second thought, nope. She didn't want to know that, either. What he thought of her was completely irrelevant. A guy like this—perfect in every way down to the high-gloss tips of his loafers—couldn't appreciate a girl like her. Even if he liked what he saw, he wouldn't like how she behaved. M. J. Rooney played a man's sport, and she wasn't afraid to speak her mind. She already caught enough flack about that from her family. She didn't need to add another disapproving man to the mix.

"Knock, knock." Dr. Ridge stood in the doorway. "Go find your own patients," he directed at Dr. Sexy. "Better yet, go get some pizza before I finish it off."

Dr. Sexy smiled again as he nodded, exuding a nonchalance that had M. J.'s muscles bunching, bracing against the attraction.

"Miss Rooney," he said. "It was nice to see you again."

It was, wasn't it? Even if she didn't remember seeing him the first time.

Chapter Three

Tag bit into a piece of portabella and prosciutto pizza while he took a seat on a wheeled stool in the exam room turned cafeteria.

So … Miss Rooney played football. That had to be a first. In this profession, he'd met people from all walks of life—D-1 football players, ultra-marathoners, prima ballerinas, heck, even a lumberjack—but a female professional football player was something new. Different. Intriguing. She didn't look anything like what he'd expect a female professional football player to look like, which was much bigger, burlier, even—dare he say—man-like. That was kind of ignorant wasn't it? But it was the truth. Stereotypes existed whether one liked to admit to them or not.

Tag spent most of his life trying not to admit the negative things.

Reaching into his front coat pocket, he pulled out his reading glasses and then his phone so he could type "Rooney Cleveland Clash" into the Google search window. The image results showed a woman who was as stunning in pictures as she was in person.

He tapped on the first picture, one of her in full equipment with her helmet wedged against her hip. She wore her chestnut-color hair long and loose over one shoulder, which was exaggerated by pads, while the other shoulder touted an embroidered "C." Those clear, blue eyes pierced the veil of reality, making him feel like she was staring back at him.

An unexpected rush of adrenaline quickened his heartbeat.

Shaking his head, Tag took another bite of his pizza. Miss Rooney was attractive, but she wasn't his type. Not even close. The don't-mess-with-me look on her beautiful face told him she would chew up and spit out anyone who stood in her way. Way too much trouble. He liked his edges clean.

"Good afternoon, Dr. Howard."

Anastasia Croft, a department administrator, stood in the doorway dressed as flawlessly usual in a pastel, monochromatic suit, with her blonde hair pulled tight into a bun. *Clean edges ... and great legs, too.*

"Anastasia." Tag smiled and dropped his phone into his pocket as he stood. "This is a nice surprise. Could I interest you in a slice of pizza?" He held up what was left of his and pointed to the box. "I owe you a rain check on our lunch the other day."

Her smile was warm but small, the picture of poise. "You're sweet, but no. If I let you tempt me with pizza today, I'll have to forego cake at my nephew's birthday party. So, you see, caving would make me a terrible aunt."

"It would also make you human."

She laughed, the sound brief but perfectly pleasant. He liked her. This was the uncomplicated kind of woman he was looking for, and she'd be a great distraction over the weekend when he was worried about seeing Jordon and Grey on Monday.

"Could I tempt you with drinks on Saturday night?"

"I'm sorry. Saturday is the party, but ... Friday I have tickets to a little ballet fundraiser. Could I tempt you into accompanying me?"

"I have game coverage," he said, sincerely disappointed. It was too bad her weekend schedule couldn't be flipped around.

"That's terribly sad." But she didn't look upset. "Another time."

"Definitely."

He'd seek her out again, because polished, professional Anastasia Croft was exactly the kind of woman he imagined bringing home to his polished, professional parents.

As he watched her walk away, Tag succumbed to more thoughts about Jordon and Grey. He could cancel the appointment, but he wouldn't. Professionally, there was too much at stake. He'd been looking for the perfect, high profile candidate to carry his research into the spotlight, and Grey could be that man. Tag would look at the injured hand, and he would treat it if possible, but he had no intention of acknowledging their genetic connection or opening up his personal life to his brothers.

Tag was a Howard. End of story.

Stuffing the crust into his mouth, he snatched the glasses off his face and returned them along with his phone to his pocket. As he stood for another piece, Dave Ridge stopped him.

"Whoa. How many have you had?"

Tag chuckled. "You wish. The rest of this is mine."

"Yeah. Yeah. I suppose I can share."

"Pizza, but not patients, right?" Tag asked, remembering Dave's joke while they were in the room with Miss Rooney. "I'll have you know I saw her first."

Dave stood on the other side of the exam table lined with food and picked up a breadstick. "I don't think so, chief. I've been seeing M. J. Rooney—in a completely clinical sense," he smiled, "since the season started. That's long before she fell over the railing and onto your precious baseball field."

M. J. Maya Jane. The night of her accident she'd told him she hated the long version of her name. He had the sudden urge to know why.

"Is she still here?" Tag asked.

"Nope. She's asymptomatic, so I gave her the progressive return-to-play plan and sent her on her way. She's the trainer's trouble now, and believe me, she's trouble. Hates a man with 'doctor' before his name. Thinks he's out to get her off the field." Dave stuck the breadstick between his lips and let it dangle from his mouth like a cigar.

Under different circumstances Tag wouldn't mind being "out to get" M. J. Rooney. He bit back the completely inappropriate words. "She plays football, huh?"

"Football." Dave gave his head an emphatic nod, setting the breadstick wagging.

Tag grinned. "Is she any good?"

"Shit." He ripped the breadstick from his mouth. "Rooney has a rocket for an arm, I'm telling you. You should come to a game. Whatever you're thinking it will be like, I can guarantee you'd be wrong."

Tag didn't mind being proven wrong when he was wrong, and he was curious enough to make him interested in the idea. "When's their next home game?"

"Saturday," Dave said, backing toward the door. "Come keep me company on the sidelines. If you're lucky, maybe you'll get to see a shoulder dislocation."

It wasn't like Tag had other plans … and he wanted plans. Still, sideline coverage was something he could take or leave. All those raging emotions and yelling coaches weren't appealing.

"We'll see," he said, although his mind was ninety-nine percent already in favor of passing on the opportunity. The other one percent wouldn't mind seeing Miss Rooney in a pair of football pants. His phone vibrated, and holding it at just the right distance from his face he saw it was his office calling.

"Hello."

"Dr. Howard, it's Tammy. I wanted you to know we've added a patient onto your end-of-day next Monday. Grey Kemmons. His agent said he spoke to you this afternoon."

Tag knew this was coming, so why did it knock the wind out of him?

He dragged a hand over his face and nodded. "Sounds good. Thanks."

Seven days until he saw his brother again. How much could one man obsess about one thing in one week? Tag didn't want to find out.

Stepping out of the exam room, he saw Dave about to walk into the room across the hall. "I'll go," Tag said, even though he still wasn't convinced he wanted to stand on the sidelines, but whether he liked it or not, he'd be coming face-to-face with his past next Monday. Facing another piece of that past by stepping foot on a field again, making it twice in one week, would be good practice—and a chance to see the blue-eyed enigma up close and personal again.

Dave smiled. "I knew you couldn't stay away."

Maybe something good would come of it.

• • •

Even though M. J. managed two full-contact practices before game day, she was abnormally nervous. What if she hadn't gotten in enough snaps? On that first on-field day after the concussion, dropping back to pass and scrambling had rattled her brain and hollowed out her stomach, but she'd powered through it, and, more importantly, she hadn't told the trainer. She wasn't stupid. If she complained of the slightest thing, nobody was going to let her set foot on the field today.

Fortunately, by the end of the week, she was really and truly symptom free, much to her father's dismay. In a rare phone call made to specifically talk about football, he'd begged M. J. to reconsider playing this season. *A brain is a terrible thing to waste.* Maybe it would've been touching had it come from a place of concern for her health, but she knew better.

In her own last-ditch effort to stop her from playing, Felicia had taken her to lunch yesterday. "Honey, women just shouldn't play football," she'd said. "We're not supposed to be that aggressive." Really? Tell that to Tanya's family, who'd had flowers delivered to the locker room before the home opener with a card that read: *To our beautiful barbarian. Kick some ass.*

Must be nice to have support like that.

M. J. slammed her locker shut. *Use it, Rooney.* All that bottled frustration was good motivation to tear up the field.

"It feels like a record-passing day," she said to her favorite target, wide receiver Jillian Bell, swatting her ass as she passed.

"I like it," Jillian yelled.

The exchange charged them up, and the locker room chatter spilled out onto the field, which was good, because the crowd was sparse, and there was nothing worse than taking the field to the sound of crickets chirping. A championship would put more people in the seats, and maybe someday they could move out of this rinky-dink, former high school stadium.

Running across the field to the sideline, she embraced the pressure to make it to the playoffs.

"How you feeling, Rooney?" Coach slapped a large hand atop her right shoulder.

"Like the D. C. defense doesn't have a chance."

"Thatta girl." He patted her arm twice. "But, you might want to come up with something more convincing for Revis. He says he's keeping a close eye on you."

M. J. rolled her eyes. As far as trainers went, Kyle Revis was a good guy who knew his stuff. He also happened to be a stickler for regulations.

"Be straight with him," Coach said. "He takes his job seriously."

"So do I."

"Hey, Rooney."

Speak of the devil. M. J. turned to see Revis flanked by Dr. Ridge and the man with the sexy smile that waltzed into her clinic exam room, Dr. Sexy. He grinned, and she had to look away before she grinned, too.

There was no room for grinning on a pre-game sideline, especially at a potential enemy. They stood in a straight line like a veritable threat of medical power. Three of them! All with the authority to pull her from the game.

"How's the head?" Revis asked.

"Still attached to my shoulders." M. J. lifted her helmet and with a tug on the earpieces to widen the base, and slid it on.

"I'm watching you," he said, creating a "V" with two fingers and pointing them at his eyes. "Dr. Ridge and Dr. Howard will be watching you, too."

So *that* was his name.

"Watch away, boys." She glanced at the other men, careful not to linger too long on Dr. Howard. Even the split second she devoted to him heated her face, making her thankful she had a substantial facemask for cover. "It'd be a shame to miss a moment of my record-breaking game."

Revis laughed. Maybe the others did, too. M. J. didn't hang around to find out. She turned and trotted onto the field for warm-ups, determined to silence them all with her performance.

After the coin toss and a twenty-yard kick-off return, M. J. took the field for the first play of the game.

"Postman," she said to the faces staring her down in the huddle.

Nobody blinked, and moments later, when the ball hit M. J.'s hands and she dropped back to pass, enough electricity rocketed through her to light the whole damn city.

Her release was quick, but not quick enough to spare her from the freight train hit to her left side. *CeCe.* She smiled as she hit the ground, knowing instinctively that the pass had been good and Jillian was already in the end zone.

When M. J. returned to the sideline, Revis was waiting for her with his doctor cronies close behind. "That was a hard hit," he said.

"That was a perfect pass," she countered.

"M. J., look at me."

Yeah. Yeah. He wanted to see her eyes and have a meaningful conversation that included questions to flush out a concussion. Not today.

She pushed past him and looked at Dr. Howard instead. His eyes were so wide she nearly laughed. Was he shocked by the way she was treating Revis, or was he impressed by the touchdown pass? Either way, the guy needed to get out more.

By halftime, the Clash was up 35-10, and M. J.'s arm was on fire—the good way. Better yet, Revis had stopped following her around the sidelines every time she wasn't in play.

Then, with nine minutes left in the fourth quarter and M. J. just twenty passing yards away from breaking her personal best, she threw a thirty-yard bomb to Janie Prior. The final score: 56-17. Clash for the win.

Jacked up on adrenaline, M. J. returned to the buzzing locker room where she showered and dressed for her shift at the bar. Normally she didn't work on game day, but the concussion set her back a few shifts, and she needed the paycheck.

"Now that's what I call an ass-kicking," Tanya said, taking the bouquet of roses off the top shelf of her locker. "You done good, girl. Despite your marshmallow head."

M. J. gave her a loving punch in the upper arm. "My head is fine."

"Debatable, but your arm is beastly." Tanya leaned in for a hug. "Maybe we'll stop by the bar after dinner."

M. J. nodded. "That would be nice." Spending time with Tanya's sports-obsessed family was always a boost to her ego.

They walked out together, despite the little pang of jealousy M. J. always got when she had to face the lack of support from her own family. Sure enough, Tanya's crew of eight, including her father, mother, sisters, brothers, and nephews, waited outside the field house door. All around M. J., Clash players met up with loving family and friends. With a roll of her shoulders and a lift of her chin, she walked through the crowd amid congratulations for a game well played. Those accolades felt good, so she focused on them.

Smiling back, M. J. said "thank you" every few steps, until she reached the outer edge of the crowd and came face to face with Dr. Howard. Maybe he was waiting for Dr. Ridge to finish up in the training room. But the flutter in her chest made her wonder.

"Miss Rooney," he said, inclining his head in an old-fashioned way that broadened her smile.

"Dr. Howard," she replied. Before the game, she refused herself permission to really look at him, but after a win like that she was entitled to a little perusal.

Letting her bag slide off her shoulder to the ground, she took him in. His long-ish hair looked like he'd pulled his hands through it a time or two. His green golf shirt brought out the gold in his eyes, and the fit was a bit more snug than what she was used to on a man—not that she was complaining. Underneath that shirt lurked a defined chest and flat abs. He was fit, but in a practical sort of way, one that said he went for quality workouts rather than lunkhead quantity. She saw way too much of the latter at the gym.

"That was an impressive passing display," he said.

"Thank you."

He slipped his hands into the pockets of his khaki pants. "Where'd you learn to throw like that?"

"Recess."

He chuckled. The sound played in the air between them, giving each breath an effervescent quality.

"What? It's true. I got hit with a football in the side of the head, and when I threw it back, it was a perfect spiral. They wouldn't leave me alone after that. I had to play."

His eyes smiled, while his lips twisted into something so sexy her knees gave the slightest buckle.

"So now what?" he asked.

"We beat Baltimore next week—in Baltimore, which is no easy feat. They're hard to read."

His smile blazed. "Do you ever think about anything other than football?"

It definitely wouldn't be appropriate to tell him she was now wondering what he looked like naked.

"I meant, what are you off to do now?"

Was he asking her out? M. J.'s mouth opened and closed, before she could shake off the stupor. "I … have to work."

"Isn't this your work?"

"My life's work, yes, but it hardly pays all the bills. Now see, if I were a man, I'd be worth millions. I hate that."

"Where do you work?"

If he weren't so pretty, she'd be annoyed by all these questions. "I'm a bartender at Mama Mary's."

He nodded like he didn't have a clue where that was, which was probably true considering his social stature. Then again, maybe he was unimpressed by her lack of respectable profession. Bartending was a crime as far as people like her father were concerned. And Dr. Howard, as sexy as he was, looked cut from the same sort of privileged cloth.

None of it mattered. He might be hot, but she wasn't looking for the slightest in-season distraction. She needed all her attention on the field if she wanted to break records and win championships.

"I gotta get going," she said, returning her bag to her shoulder.

"Of course. Maybe I'll see you around."

"Maybe." Although, the odds might be better than "maybe" considering how many times she'd bumped into him since she fell.

"Can I call you, M. J.?"

"You can call me anything but Maya Jane."

His smile unglued her. "I meant can I call you on the phone sometime, maybe take you out to dinner?"

"Oh." It was hard to feel silly for the misunderstanding when he was looking at her like she was water for a parched man. He was so damn tempting. "I'm flattered. I am. It's just that I don't date during the season."

"And you hate doctors."

Well, there was that, too. Wait. How did he know that? Had she said that on the field after she fell? She wished she could remember. She hated being at a disadvantage.

"I *avoid* doctors," she corrected. "They like to keep me out of the game."

He stepped closer. "Maybe you've been spending too much time with the wrong doctors."

She didn't even know what to say to that. "Dr. Howard, I …"

"Tag. Call me Tag. Then maybe you won't be reminded I'm a doctor."

She smiled, but it was guarded, because this whole exchange was unexpected. "Fine. I'll call you Tag."

"Then you're going to need my phone number."

A laugh broke free. "You know what I meant."

"I do."

"I really have to go." She stood there in silence several seconds longer than she had to, looking him in the shiny green eyes, wishing beyond all common sense that she had a few hours to waste on him. It could be fun. Then again, it could be a nightmare—one that compromised her concentration and sent her season into a tailspin.

She couldn't afford that. It was football first.

She had way too much to prove.

Chapter Four

Two days later, he sat in his office still bothered by the fact that M. J. had brushed him off, despite her very valid reason for doing so. She wanted to focus on football, not satisfy his curiosity about an attraction to a woman who was not at all his type. Tag couldn't even believe he asked her for her number in the first place. That wasn't his initial plan. He'd simply been waiting for Dave to finish meeting with the coach. Seeing M. J. was a bonus, and the minute he was in her presence, he knew he wanted to see her again.

If the only way to make that happen was to go to another game, then so be it. Watching her was like being hypnotized. It wasn't until halftime when she disappeared into the locker room that Tag even realized he'd been standing on the field for ninety minutes without a single uptick in his heart rate.

M. J. Rooney was magical, and she was smart, too. Turning him down was the right thing to do. Asking her out had been completely uncharacteristic of him, and if she'd said yes, he might not have followed through. Attraction was a small part of the relationship equation. *Clean edges*, Tag reminded himself. He had all the messiness he could handle waiting in exam room C.

He hit the heel of his palm against the center of his forehead and exhaled. *Time to get a move on.* He'd already procrastinated as long as he could, staring at his laptop and thinking about M. J.. At this point, Tag just needed to get Grey's appointment over with, so life could get back to normal.

When Tag finally made the death march down the carpeted hallway toward the exam, his physician's assistant, Leanne, was waiting for him.

"Ready, Doc?" she asked, all wide-eyed and enthusiastic. Why shouldn't she be? She had no idea what she was walking into.

Tag smiled, even though the expression was hollow, and he tried to take some solace in the fact that Leanne would be in the room. Some might construe it as cowardice, a buffer between Tag and the truth, but he preferred to look at it as keeping things professional.

With a sharp inhale and a tilt of his head, Tag pushed into the room.

He wasn't sure what he expected. Although it'd been twenty-five years since he'd seen either Jordon or Grey in person, somehow he expected those younger versions to be waiting for him.

They weren't.

He recognized the grown men, one sitting on the exam table, the other standing near the sink. He'd seen their pictures on television and online by accident or in moments of weakness, but there was an odd sense of disconnect that surrounded him right now, and it acted like a bubble of protection. They were just men, nothing more.

"Good afternoon," Tag managed, purposefully leaving off their names. *That* might pop the bubble.

Jordon and Grey were equally hesitant to speak, nodding instead.

"This is my PA, Leanne Jenkins. She's been involved with my research since the start, so I thought it was prudent for her to be here."

Leanne, oblivious to the monumental moment unfolding before her, leaned forward for handshakes. She made small talk while Tag maneuvered past Jordon to the sink. As he washed his hands, he breathed deeper than he'd allowed himself since entering the room. *So far so good.* If the rest of the exam continued this way, Tag had nothing to fear.

He faced Grey, but refused to make eye contact. "Let's take a look at that hand."

Grey unwound the bandage, and the minute Tag saw the wound, his thoughts anchored on medicine. "Okay. First, I'm going to have to check and see how deep it is."

Leanne held out a steel tray, and Tag pinched a long-stem swab from the line-up of supplies. Gripping the swab end of the stick, he slid his other hand beneath Grey's right arm.

"It's going to be a little uncomfortable, but I'll be quick." Normally, Tag would look at the patient to ascertain his or her mental state before he proceeded. The last thing he needed was to have the arm jerked away in panic. But at the precise moment his gaze began a slow crawl upward, Jordon placed a supportive hand on Grey's shoulder.

The show of solidarity crushed Tag—the odd man out. He'd always been. He spread the wound just a bit and stuck the stick end of the swab into it, measuring the depth.

Other than a low growl, Grey tolerated the procedure well.

"Not too deep. A couple millimeters," Tag said, mostly for Leanne's benefit.

"Is that good?"

Tag glanced at Jordon. "It is. That, coupled with the fact the edges look good and it's not draining too much means infection isn't likely and there's an adequate blood supply. Those are all things I need to see in order to re-grow tissue. I do want to study the most recent lab work and cultures. You brought those, correct?"

"It's right here," Leanne said, pulling a piece of paper from the chart and handing it to Tag.

He took it on reflex. If he'd thought about it, he'd have asked her what the values were, because now he was faced with either struggling to interpret the document without his reading glasses, or sucking it up and pulling them out of his pocket like he would at any other time with any other patient.

Just like that his *so far so good* became an *oh, damn*. Tag's vision had been too big of an issue growing up for Jordon and Grey not to be reminded by the simple act of him sliding on his bifocals.

Taking the paper and facing the counter, Tag waited until he had his back to them to reach into his pocket and slide on the glasses.

"Are you blind?" His biological father's words echoed in his head. "Can you not see that ball?"

Tag's chest squeezed, and he struggled to breathe through the pain while he tried to decipher the original doctor's chicken scratch from Grey's chart.

"He's not blind," he heard a much younger version of Grey say. "It's just fuzzy."

This time when Tag's chest squeezed he raised a fist to press against his breastbone. There was no way he was going to be able to access this information in a timely manner with his head full of ghosts.

Tag clawed at his face, removing the glasses, and then he faced Leanne. "You know what? I'm going to have to make a few phone calls before I can make a solid determination. It looks promising. It does." He glanced at the men, but returned his focus to Leanne. "I'm going to head back to my office. Why don't you re-dress the wound and tell them a little about the procedure we might use? And then … I'll be in touch."

Even though Tag was walking down the hall, he breathed like he was sprinting.

"Hey."

Jordon's voice stopped Tag in his tracks, but he couldn't bring himself to turn around.

"I know this can't be easy, Tag, so from the bottom of my heart, thank you, man."

The pain in Tag's chest pushed into his throat, and his eyes burned with tears. Lame or not, he simply lifted a hand in a sort-of wave and called out a gravelly, "You bet," before he continued his escape down the hall.

For twenty-five years, Tag had imagined his biological family, living it up without him—the ball and chain around their baseball dreams. What would dear old dad think if he knew part of that dream now literally rested in the hands of his blind, little, sissy boy?

The irony was paralyzing.

Somehow Tag managed to pull himself together and look over Grey's medical records. He had a coherent conversation with the doctor who'd been in charge of Grey's rehabilitation, too. Then, Tag stayed in his office much longer than he normally would have, hoping and praying Jordon and Grey were long gone, back to Pittsburgh. When he finally stuck his head outside his office, the cleaning crew was hard at work.

"Late night, Doc. Glad to see you're finally heading home."

Tag nodded, but the idea of driving home, where he would sit in an empty condo with nothing but thoughts about his day to hound him, wasn't appealing. Under the pressure of normal work-related stress, he'd consider stopping off at his parents for a little detox and clarity—and a Goose and tonic with the man who'd introduced him to top-shelf liquor. But not tonight. They would know something was wrong, and this wasn't something he wanted to share with them. He never wanted his parents to see him as anything other than their successful son.

Tag wouldn't go back to what he'd been.

As he hit the on-ramp toward home, he contemplated stopping at the country club for a couple drinks, but he'd done that almost every night this week. Surely, someone was going to start worrying he had a drinking problem. He didn't. He stared at the alcohol in the glass more than he drank it. Still, it couldn't look good to the casual observer, especially those who knew him professionally.

What he needed was neutral territory, someplace no one cared about him or his problems ... someplace like Mama Mary's. The place came to mind as he spied a highway sign announcing the community college turn-off two miles ahead. From what he'd heard, Mary's was just off campus. The dive bar was nowhere near his usual scene. Heck, the neighborhood had been enough to keep him away even when his med-school friends wanted some of Mary's almost-famous pulled pork.

Maybe M. J. was working. The possibility was enough to get him to the parking lot. Now, if he could just find the nerve to get out of the car and go inside.

•••

M. J. dropped a cherry into an old fashioned and set the cocktail in front of the guy at the back corner of the bar.

"Much obliged," he said, tipping a non-existent hat.

She smiled as she gathered the dollar bills off the counter. The minute she faced the register, she stifled a yawn with the back of her hand. The quiet, Monday-night crowd wasn't enough to offset the exhaustion from practice that afternoon.

Mona passed the bar, empty tray in hand, on her way to the kitchen. "Can you pour me the biggest cup of coffee you can find?" M. J. dragged a few quarters up the curving plastic until they hit her palm.

"Of course."

She was going to pay for the influx of caffeine into her normally pristine in-season bloodstream, but falling asleep, hugging the register wasn't going to go over well with the boss, even if the boss was Tanya's mom.

Turning with the old guy's change in hand, M. J. dropped the coins at her feet when she saw the face smiling back at her from the far end of the bar. Apparently she wasn't going to need that coffee to liven up her evening after all.

Dr. Howard appears again.

She bent and retrieved the change, passing it off to its rightful owner with a "thank you" and a smile, and then she walked to the other end of the bar.

"Surprised?" Tag asked.

"And confused. You don't seem like the kind of guy who frequents this neighborhood." She slid a cocktail napkin in front of him.

"Now what makes you say that?"

She eyed him up a little too long, taking in his professional but chaotic appearance. That silky hair was begging for a comb … or fingers. Hers twitched like the traitors they were.

"Do you see any other suits and ties around here?" she asked, stepping aside, giving him an unobstructed view of the dingy surroundings and the handful of down-on-their-luck patrons who were hanging around on a Monday evening.

"Yeah, well, underneath this suit and tie, I'm just like them." He sort of choked on a low chuckle. When he did, something darkened his eyes, and the wrinkles on his forehead deepened.

"What's your poison?" she asked, figuring this surprise visit was just as confusing to him. "I'm afraid our draft selection is a little lowbrow."

"Do you have Grey Goose?"

She laughed. "We have vodka, and occasionally it's a little gray, but I don't think it has anything to do with geese."

"Okay, then I'll take a gray vodka tonic without the goose, and a lime, please."

God, he was cute, out-of-place and bothered by something she couldn't help but wonder about—something that brought him here. She didn't know whether that should flatter or scare her.

M. J.'s stomach gave a turn, and her head followed. She grabbed the edge of the counter to keep steady, but masked the motion with the reach of her other hand toward the vodka bottle. Why was she always so attracted to the lost cause?

Busying herself with the drink, she tried not to think about Tag sitting at the end of the bar, clearly there to see her. But when she set the drink in front of him and watched him take a good long sip, she couldn't contain her curiosity.

"What brings you here?"

He poked at the floating lime with the cocktail straw. "I've always heard bartenders are good listeners."

She'd heard that before, too, from any number of guys hitting on her, but coming from Tag in a quiet voice, it seemed like more of a plea than a line.

Turning to the man at the other end of the bar, she called out a quick, "Are you good?" and when he nodded, settled her attention on Tag. "Bad day?"

"The worst." He tossed back the rest of the drink like it was water. "Refill?" He jiggled the ice in the empty glass.

She took the tumbler and filled it again, all the while wondering what constituted "the worst" day for a doctor. Having a patient die was her best guess.

Sliding the glass in front of him, she rested her elbows on the edge of the bar. "What happened?"

"I can't really say. HIPPA privacy laws and all that."

M. J. nodded. "Did somebody die? Can you tell me that much?"

"Nobody died."

"That's good."

"That is good."

She watched him drink, liking the way his shiny eyes rolled over her face as he did. Even downtrodden, he was sexy.

He set the tumbler on the bar and rose up on his elbows, narrowing the space between them enough that she could smell the spice of his cologne and the liquor on his breath. She liked that, too. More than she should. He was clearly more complicated than what would be good for her—even if she weren't in-season.

"Do you have family?" he asked, stabbing the cocktail straw straight through the lime.

"Of course, I do. I didn't just hatch."

His brows lifted, but his gaze didn't leave the glass. "Hatching would be nice."

Maybe professional woes didn't bring him here, after all. "You don't like your family?"

"Depends on which one you're talking about."

Shit. He was married. She never even thought to ask. She pushed off the bar and stepped back. "You don't like your in-laws?"

That got him to look at her, a gaze that started low on her chin and swept over her face until he was smiling, all crooked and cocky. "I don't have in-laws. I'm not married. Do you really think I would've asked for your number if I was?"

She shrugged. "Some guys would. Hell, I was propositioned right here by a guy whose wife was in the ladies room. In this line of work, I see it all." She lifted his empty glass. "Would you like another?"

His lips hitched, and his sparkling eyes stayed locked on hers. "I'd like a lot of things, but, yeah, we can start with that."

She swallowed a rush of attraction, snatched his glass, and moved toward the vodka, maintaining eye contact. This was one guy she shouldn't turn her back on. He had a way of sneaking up on her and testing her usual resolve. Half-a-dozen, watered-down, vodka tonics later, M. J.'s shift was over, and Tag was still at the bar. Now what was she supposed to do? He'd had enough liquor to make her think he might not be in any shape to drive, and she couldn't leave him here, which was clearly outside his comfort zone, to fend for himself, so she shrugged into her jean jacket, rounded the bar and stood at his side. "How 'bout we take a walk?"

A stroll around the block would buy her some time, and it might scare the liquor right out of him when they passed the three-hundred-pound former drug dealer who was now a bouncer at JR's.

"Are you asking me out, Miss Rooney?"

"Out of this bar? Yes, I am. Somebody has to protect you."

Tag slipped off the stool and came to stand far too close to feel innocent. "You really are unorthodox, aren't you?"

Heat slithered along her spine and rooted between her legs. "Why, Dr. Howard, that's the nicest thing anyone's ever said to me."

Which was problematic. A woman like M. J. could get addicted to compliments that celebrated her unconventional ways. And addictions were dangerous.

She'd have to remember that, especially when he was smiling.

Chapter Five

Tag looked at the glossy black paint of his BMW 7 series, sparkling in the glow of security lights. Next to where he parked was what looked like an old, rusted newspaper box, sporting layers of graffiti. "Are you sure it's safe to leave my car here?"

M. J. was already walking away from the bar parking lot to the crumbling sidewalk. "You sound like my father." By the huff in her voice it wasn't a compliment. "You don't get out of those golden-gated suburbs much, do you?"

Tag jogged to catch up with her. A minute ago, he'd considered arguing the necessity of this mercy mission. Contrary to her belief, he didn't need protection, and he wasn't drunk—thanks to the watered-down vodka tonics she was pushing on him—but he wanted to be with her, so he'd play along. Maybe she was taking him back to her place. After the day he'd had, he wouldn't argue with that.

"You don't even know where I live." Still, Tag couldn't help but wish this sidewalk *was* in his well-lit, chronically safe neighborhood. He glanced at the derelict surroundings and moved closer to her. She looked fierce, striding down the sidewalk in the moonlight—a veritable goddess—and he had the distinct impression nobody would mess with him when M. J. was around, which was just the sort of weak-ass thing his biological father would expect him to say.

M. J.'s little comment about someone having to protect him didn't seem so innocent anymore.

"I bet I can guess where you live," she said.

"I'll save you the trouble ..." and him the slight annoyance of hearing her list every swanky neighborhood in town. "Shaker Heights."

She chuckled. "Probably would've been my second or third guess."

The streetlight overhead cut out suddenly, and the path plunged into a deeper darkness. He didn't want to be a complete jerk and ask about the safety of this area again, but the hairs standing up on the back of his neck did not make him feel comfortable. And Tag hated being uncomfortable.

"Where are we going?" It was a better option for assessing the true danger he was in.

"End of the block. My friend's family owns a gym."

"A gym?"

"Yep. It's my normal routine after a shift. I walk down here to Bruiser's, work out a bit, and then Tanya and I walk home. In case you haven't noticed there's not much going on around here other than boozing, and it's not a great idea for anyone to walk alone."

As if on cue, they neared a dingy building with a neon beer sign in the front window. A massive, intimidating man scowled as they approached.

"Evening, Hank," M. J. called out as she stepped into the faint glow of a streetlight that wasn't burnt out or shattered.

The man actually smiled, taxing though it seemed to be for him.

"My friend, Doc," she said, flicking a wrist toward Tag.

The big guy grunted a greeting.

"Have a nice night," Tag said as they continued on their way.

She was looking at him again, studying him really. A slow smile lit up her face as they walked away from the giant bouncer man and ominous bar into a far more ominous darkness. Surprisingly, Tag had begun to care less and less about his surroundings, concentrating only on M. J., admiring her easy beauty. No makeup, no pretention, no shield. It was … refreshing.

"You don't mind if I call you Doc, do you?"

"No. That's fine."

"Good, because every time I think to call you Tag I want to follow it up with 'you're it.'" She grinned.

"Like I haven't heard that one before."

"Is it short for something?"

Shit. He looked away, followed a line of missing siding on the building to his right. "Taggard."

She made a considering sound deep in her throat. "Unusual."

"Yep." More lights and noises up ahead. He hoped it was their destination and therefore the end of this conversation. He'd come to M. J. tonight to avoid thoughts about his family. He didn't want to dive head-first back into that mess. "Is that where we're going?" he asked, hoping to hurry along the subject change.

"It is." She nodded. "Is there a story behind a name like Taggard?"

He should've known she wouldn't give up. He might not know her well, but her tenacity was clear.

Tag sucked in a mouthful of musty air. "Taggard was my mother's maiden name." His biological mother, but he wasn't going there. No way.

"Cool," she said.

It was his turn. "What's the deal with Maya Jane?"

She glared at him, but then softened the stare with another smile. "Honestly, it's too much of a mouthful for me, and it represents someone somebody else wants me to be. I'm no Maya Jane. I'm M. J."

Tag would have to agree. The shorter version suited her no-nonsense attitude.

She nodded at a couple of guys sporting hooded sweatshirts and standing alongside a metal door decorated with graffiti and the name Buster's Gym and Ring.

Sure enough, there was a boxing ring in the middle of the rundown establishment, and if Tag thought the air outside left something to be desired, the air inside was fouler than the locker room after a hockey game. Good thing he was used to the stench of athletic success.

"Chica, you're wearing my favorite boots." A short, fat man with a baseball cap too high on his head and a grin splitting his moon-pie face walked toward M. J.

She glanced down at the boots Tag was just now getting a good look at. Shiny black. Knee-high. Miles and miles of laces up the back. *Damn.* He rubbed at a hot spot beneath his breast.

"Yep." M. J. bent down and kissed the man on the cheek.

"You know why I like them boots?"

"I do."

"Because they're for ass kicking," they said in unison, laughing at the end.

Tag didn't know what to make of the scene, or the older man. His lack of athletic physique paired with advanced age and a white towel over the shoulder seemed to indicate he was some sort of manager.

"This is my friend, Doc. Doc, this is Pop. He's my best friend's father, and this ..." she swept her arm to the side, "is his gym."

"Nice to meet ya, Doc." The man had a vice grip for a handshake. He eyed up Tag good and long. "You box?"

"No, sir."

"We're going to change that."

Tag's eyes widened enough to bring another laugh to M. J.'s lips.

"No, Pop. He's not from around here. We just wanted to stop by and see T spar."

"Oh, I know he's not from around here dressed all spiffy like that." The older man chuckled. "But that doesn't mean he's not welcome in my ring. Whaddya say?"

"Dad!" The shout came from across the room where a giant of a woman in electric blue headgear hung long arms over the top ring rope. Her hands were dressed in purple boxing gloves. When

Pop turned, the woman must've caught sight of M. J., because she slammed her gloves together, fist to fist, and let out a whoop. "I was about to give up on you. Figured you went home to bed."

"And miss this?" M. J. asked as she walked closer to the ring. "No way."

"Hey, you look familiar." One purple glove poked in Tag's direction.

There were other people milling around the dusty warehouse-sized space, and after that, all of them were looking at him. Tag flashed a smile despite the complete uneasiness stuffing up his stomach. This was unlike any place he'd ever been. Raw, gritty, and full of people who looked highly skeptical of his motives, considering he was dressed in a suit.

"That's Doc. He was on the sideline for Saturday's game." M. J. snatched him around the elbow and pulled him closer. "Everyone," she yelled, "this is Doc. Doc, this is everyone."

More grunts, and then a young man with a flash of angry red below his left eye stepped into view. "Doc as in, ya know, doctor?"

"Yep." Tag squinted to get a better look at the abrasion on the kid's face.

"You, uh, wanna take a look at somethin' for me?" He was maybe sixteen, skinny, with the biggest tattoo covering his pencil neck.

Tag's instincts said no freaking way did he want to take a look at anything this kid was dealing with. He had "trouble" and "mess" written all over him.

"Dante, he's not here to work," M. J. chimed in.

And that was true, but a jagged part of Tag forced a smile at the kid. "Is it your eye?"

The kid nodded.

"How'd that happen?" Tag asked, stepping closer, letting his curiosity get the best of him.

He shrugged. "It, uh, rubs on the headgear. I mean it did, and it was little at first, and then it got worse."

"Did you see anybody for it?"

"Nah. Shit. I got no insurance, and that clinic's never open anymore. You know I cleaned it out real good a couple times, but that's it."

Turning toward M. J. first, but spying Pop hoisting himself between the ropes, Tag took a few steps toward the ring. "Excuse me, do you have a training room?" The minute he asked, Tag knew it was a stupid question. This place was lucky to have a water fountain.

"The whole place is for training," Pop said.

M. J. stepped closer to the ring. "He's talking about a place where people can go get fixed up and wrapped."

"Ain't got one of those."

"How about a sink and some antibacterial soap?" Tag asked.

"I got a sink in the bathroom." Pop pointed to the far wall. "Don't know about soap, though."

Tag wouldn't touch the kid until he was reasonably sterile, and he had a feeling the bathroom wasn't going to cut it as far as cleanliness was concerned, but then he remembered the sideline bag he carried in the trunk of his car. He had everything he needed in there.

"I'm going to run to my car for a minute. I have some supplies in the trunk. I'll be right back." A man distracted by a medical mission, Tag turned and jogged away.

"Hey," M. J. called. "You sure you don't need me to go with you?"

When he faced her, she was smiling, and that smile only added to the resurgence of Tag's confidence. "I'll be fine."

And for the first time in twenty-four hours, he felt like he would be.

• • •

M. J. sat on a box in the corner of Pop's office, having weaseled her way into the exam simply to make sure Tag and Dante didn't kill each other. She had a feeling Tag wasn't used to patients like this. Dante had a reputation for being rude and unresponsive with authority, but Pop was trying to change that, like he did with so many kids.

The walls of his cluttered, dusty office were lined with outdated snapshots of Pop with some of boxing's greats. Those photos interspersed with school pictures—some as impressive as collegiate-level sports—of the kids who'd trained here. Tanya's dad was a local legend and a hero to these boys. As the one man in M. J.'s life who encouraged her to be exactly who she was, he was a hero to M. J., too. Pop's only caveat was for her to be a better M. J. today than she was yesterday. Words to live by.

In the stillness, she watched as Tag's gloved hands examined Dante's face. Tag had removed his jacket and rolled up his sleeves. As he worked, the muscles in his back rolled against the smooth, shiny fabric of his dress shirt. She had the ridiculous desire to run her palms over his back.

"I can't know for sure until I swab it and send the culture for testing, but I don't have the capability of doing something like that here. Can you come to my office?"

Dante shook his head. "I already told ya, man. I got no insurance." The lack of respect in his address wasn't half as offensive as his sneer.

M. J. readied to intervene in case Dante's attitude prompted arrogance from Tag that would only fuel a confrontation.

"I can work around that," Tag said with nary a hint of annoyance at the boy. "In fact, I might be able to help you out with that going forward, too. I know people." He smiled, packing 75,000 watts of electricity into the easy expression.

M. J. pawed at the collar of her shirt. Hot flash. She refused to believe the heat crawling up her face had anything to do with Tag's kindness toward a kid he could just as easily suspect was capable of spray-painting the hood of his pretty little luxury car.

"Your office on the bus line?" Dante asked.

"It is, but if you have trouble getting there, you let me know. I'll figure something out there, too. We just need to get this taken care of as soon as possible."

"Pop can take me," Dante said with a lift of his chin.

And Pop would. M. J. smiled.

"Okay. Then, how about you come by my office after school tomorrow? I'll talk to Pop and make sure he's on board."

"I don't do school, but yeah, tomorrow sounds good."

Tag dragged the gloves off with a snapping sound, and M. J. held her breath, waiting for the "stay in school" lecture a professional-degree-holding guy like Tag had to be cooking up in his head. A kid like Dante wouldn't tolerate it.

"Then how 'bout you come by earlier if it works for Pop? That way we can get the results faster, because I have to tell you, no more boxing until we know what this is."

"Ah, shit. Seriously?"

"Seriously. I don't want to be the bad guy here, but if it's something contagious, then everyone is going to be at risk for it from sharing equipment. Worse, it could cause an infection in your blood, and we don't want that, because that would keep you out of the gym for a long, long time. Got me?"

Dante hung his head, but he offered up a "gotcha."

"Okay, then let's find Pop and hash this out."

Dante flashed a hard look at Tag's outstretched hand, but he took it and added, "Yeah, thanks, man."

Again M. J. yanked the collar of her shirt away from her neck. This time, she absentmindedly fanned at her face.

Dante rolled out of the room as Tag returned his supplies to his bag. He glanced at her in between rearranging boxes and zipping compartments. "You could've stayed to watch your friend box."

"I know." But then she would've missed this oddly sexy scene: a gorgeous, polished guy with a soft-hearted mission and smarts the likes of which she'd never seen. "I wanted to help if you needed me to."

He straightened with a devastating grin. "Like my bodyguard?"

Mm. Mm. Mm. The sultry images that word conjured were not good considering M. J. had already decided she wasn't interested in getting messed up with a man during this critical football season.

"I could definitely be a bodyguard. I got the ass-kicking boots, you know?" She raised a leg and pointed her toe, hoping the touch of humor would diffuse anything unseemly developing between them.

She knew she'd taken the wrong approach the minute she saw his eyes widen and linger on her leg as his grin faded.

"Believe me. I know." His voice was one breathy notch above a whisper.

"Hey, man, I brought Pop."

M. J.'s booted foot crashed to the floor the minute Dante walked into the room.

Pop ambled along behind the boy. "I can get him to you."

Tag faced the men, but not before M. J. noticed the exaggerated rise and fall of his shoulders. A calming, cooling breath, maybe? God knew after whatever just happened between them she needed a couple dozen of those, too. She tried her damnedest to fit in as many as she could while the guys discussed Dante's appointment.

Later, as they watched Tanya spar, M. J. tried to settle into her evening routine despite Tag by her side.

"Are you gloving up?" Tanya hung on the ropes when the match had ended.

M. J. glanced at Tag and shook her head. "Not tonight."

Tanya smiled. "How 'bout you, Doc?"

He laughed. "No, thanks."

"Fine. Maurice," Tanya yelled, "get your ass in this ring. And you," she jabbed toward M. J., "get out of here. Who brings a date to a boxing ring?"

"It's not a date."

Tanya looked skeptical as she backed away.

"It's not," Tag said. "She turned me down."

"And you see what good that did me." M. J. couldn't hold back her smile.

A minute later, it faltered when Tag said, "I'm going to go. I'm messing up your evening."

She shook her head. "No, you're not. I'm the one who brought you here. And I'm glad I did. I bet Dante's glad I did, too."

Tag nodded. "I'm glad I came, but I'm still going to go. I've taken up enough of your time."

M. J. followed him out onto the dark, quiet street. She figured she'd say goodnight and return to the gym, but she said, "I'll walk with you" instead.

"I can walk back on my own." He glanced at her as they headed toward his car. "Besides, if anyone's supposed to be walking anyone anywhere, it's the guy walking the girl to her car."

"Only in misogynistic fairytales. In reality, the weaker person—male or female—gets the escort. Trust me, you're weaker, especially around here."

He winced and looked away.

Shit. She'd practically called him a misogynist, and then said he was weak on top of that. Where was her filter? No wonder he'd flinched like she'd just keyed his precious Beemer. Then again, she didn't know him well enough to be reading him. Maybe underneath all the sexy grins and gazes he was really just another asshole who couldn't handle it when a woman had the balls to point out she was stronger than him.

He hadn't seemed like an asshole with Dante back at the gym.

"I was kidding," she finally managed.

"I know." He nodded as he looked ahead.

Sometimes her bravado put her at odds with other people. She didn't want that to happen after the evening they'd had and the kindness he'd shown for one of Pop's kids.

"You're not weaker than me. I mean, look, you're a good three inches taller and what, fifty pounds heavier?" She lowered her shoulder into his arm. "See? I know how to hit, and you didn't even move." As she straightened, his arm wrapped around her waist, drawing her against him, letting her feel exactly how strong he was.

"I just moved," he said, but he didn't let her go. He didn't so much as loosen up on the pressure.

Heat swirled around her waist, where his arm and hand pressed against her. When he faced her, holding her against the length of him, the sensation grew to cover every inch of her skin.

"What are you doing?" she whispered, watching shadows play across his handsome face. Her hands flattened against his chest, and her chin tilted upward.

"Trying to determine who's weaker." His gaze roved her face, always returning to her lips.

"Am I supposed to break your grip or something?" Each word was breathier than the last.

"Or something." He dropped his mouth an inch closer to hers. "See, right now I'm telling myself it would be a very bad idea to kiss you, considering you don't date during the football season. But it's really hard to stick with rational thoughts, because, honestly … those boots."

Her heart hammered in her chest. "They're just boots."

"They're kryptonite," he said, lowering his face until his lips brushed against hers. His warm breath skittered across her mouth, scattering goose pimples over her neck and chest.

Screw the test of wills. M. J. leaned into him, fusing their lips together.

With heated hands, he tipped her head and cradled her face, pulling at her lips with his, tasting her with his tongue, until she was gripping the collar of his dress shirt.

When he finally pulled back, she was woozy.

"I'd say we're about even in the weakness department," Tag said, lacing his hand with hers and continuing on their way toward his car.

M. J. couldn't see straight, let alone think. That's why she was letting him hold her hand. She opened her mouth for words or to laugh at the night's ridiculous turn of events, but she was stunned silent, her skin still buzzing.

"Can I give you a ride home?" he asked when they reached the parking lot.

"No." She backed away, because this had already gone too far. "I live close."

"How close?"

She pointed to the two floors above the bar. "That close."

"Convenient."

For work. That's probably what he meant, but the mischievous voice in her head told her it was convenient for other things, too, like finishing what they started a few minutes ago.

Tag must have noticed her confliction, because he opened the car door, and with one hand braced against the roof, readied to get inside. "I'm going to call you, M. J."

"Why?" She asked, stepping back again, because she did not trust herself.

"Because kisses like that are meant to happen again."

She choked out a laugh. "Oh, you think so?"

"I know so." He winked and sank into the driver's seat.

Dear God, she hoped he was wrong, because if one kiss had her head floating to the heavens, anything more would blow her concentration to hell.

Chapter Six

Pop wore the same tired baseball cap from the other night, and Dante wore a faded, ripped sweatshirt. They looked uncomfortable in the gleaming exam room. "I'm glad you made it," Tag said, reaching out to shake Pop's hand, hoping he could settle the discomfort with some heartfelt hospitality. To his surprise, Dante followed along with the grown-up greeting. "I got a hold of your mother this morning, and she gave me permission to treat you. Just a formality because you're underage." Dante rolled his eyes and sank into the bulky hood of his sweatshirt. "She was hoping maybe your father would bring you instead." Tag glanced at Pop, who was shaking his head emphatically while staring at a spot somewhere above Tag's head.

"No fucking way," Dante said.

That widened Tag's eyes.

"Dante," Pop snapped. "Apologize for your filthy mouth right now."

The kid stared at his feet. "Sorry, man."

"Head up and with respect," Pop countered. "This *man* is doin' you a huge favor."

"It's okay." Tag hated to see the kid chastised for something that was obviously seated pretty deep.

Dante made eye contact with Tag. "I'm sorry. I appreciate this. A lot. I just wanna get back in the ring."

Athletes, no matter how old or how decorated, always wanted the same thing. Dante's steadfast determination made Tag smile, and this smile chipped away at the heaviness of the day. It didn't matter that he had to face his brothers again tomorrow. Right now, he was going to focus on a down-on-his-luck kid, who wanted nothing more from him than medical treatment.

Twenty minutes later, Tag patted Dante on the back and handed him a bag full of free pharmaceuticals. "I'll let you know what the lab says, but I'm willing to bet it's herpes gladitorium."

Dante wasn't too keen on the diagnosis. Then again, who would be when the name involved *herpes*?

"We'll have you back in the ring in no time," Tag reassured. "Those meds will help, and I'll guide Pop as far as sanitizing equipment is concerned."

"Sounds expensive," Pop said. Even if Tag hadn't been inside the gym he'd have known by the wrinkle of Pop's nose that there wasn't money to spare.

"It doesn't have to be. Just clean everything with bleach."

"Everything? That's a lot of bleach and a lot of cleaning."

"It's my fault," Dante said. "I'll help."

The kid looked so dejected that the words jumped from Tag's mouth. "I can help, too." He had a full day here and then game coverage tonight, which made the offer a bit flimsy. "I'm pretty booked the rest of the day, but I'll figure something out."

"Thanks." This time, Dante was the one to initiate the handshake, a small token of progress that had Tag wondering if he couldn't trade game coverage with another doc, so he could spend some quality time at the gym tonight.

Then the kid asked to use the restroom, and wandered down the hall.

"I appreciate your time," Pop said, gripping Tag's hand in both of his as they stood outside the exam room.

A surge of emotion vibrated in Tag's chest, and he cleared it with a cough. "Don't mention it. He needed a doctor, and I'm a doctor. No big deal."

"It is to me," Pop said, giving Tag's hand one hell of a squeeze before he let go. "It is to him. That boy has a rough life. Not a lot of people are good to him."

Tag had already figured that out.

"That outburst about his dad," Pop continued, shaking his head. "The guy's a loser. Mean SOB. Dante's the little one in the family, and he gets pushed around. Boxing makes him feel stronger."

This was starting to hit too close to home, and the familiar need to separate from anything similar to his old life had Tag stepping back. He smoothed his tie with the palm of his hand when what he was really doing was applying pressure to stop the surge of stomach acid into his throat. "I'm glad I could help." He just needed to be more careful about how much help he gave. "I'll call his mother with the results later today or tomorrow."

"Okay."

Dante emerged from the restroom, sinking into his sweatshirt again. *The little one*, who *gets pushed around*. Tag saw the boy's torment clearly, could feel every angry word and wicked blow. He hurt all over—for himself as much as for Dante—and he wished there was a way to eradicate the pain for both of them.

"We'll see you tonight," Pop said.

Tag blinked, resting his brain. "Tonight. To sterilize equipment. Right."

He tried not to feel like a complete jerk who was suddenly thinking about bailing on a good man and a troubled kid, but self-preservation mattered, too. Tag needed to get a grip on this life he'd been carefully guarding all these years, because it was starting to elude his control. And control was the only thing keeping him from slipping out of this comfortable world the luck of the social services draw had landed him in twenty-five years ago. Nobody needed to know who he was beyond Edna and Simon Howard's son.

Tomorrow he would see his brothers again, but that contact didn't have to change him. And while stopping off to see M. J. after tonight's baseball game and then heading over to the gym to help Pop and Dante clean seemed harmless, it wasn't Tag's usual scene. He needed to stay anchored in the things that got him this comfortable life, like Edna and Simon. For the first time in twenty-five years, Tag had seen his brothers, and now here he was teetering, visiting seedy bars and boxing rings, and kissing a woman he barely knew on a sidewalk in the wrong part of town.

And until a couple minutes ago, Tag was thinking about doing it all over again.

M. J. Rooney's gritty, raw world, which was filled with kids like Dante—kids like Tag used to be—was one he escaped a long time ago. He couldn't afford to go back if he wanted to keep moving ahead.

• • •

M. J. glanced at her phone, resting on the shelf tucked beneath the register. She'd looked at it far too many times these last couple days to not be annoyed with her behavior. So what if Tag said he'd call, or that kisses like theirs were meant to be repeated? She didn't agree then, and she didn't want to agree now. It was just that the more she thought about the kiss, the more she was inclined to believe him.

Apparently, he'd had a change of heart.

She huffed as she held a pilsner glass beneath the tap and pulled the lever to release the beer. But she'd wanted it this way. She didn't want personal-life distractions compromising her play on-field. Too bad she ended up sacked twice in today's scrimmage. Both times, she'd had fleeting thoughts about whether or not Tag had called while her phone was stashed inside her locker.

So much for avoiding distraction.

After passing the beer to a patron, M. J. reached for the television remote and flipped the channel to ESPN. Listening to sports TV would get her psyched for the next game and screw her head on good and straight—unless it was sports TV that had anything to do with Cleveland's baseball team, because Cleveland's baseball team made her think of falling onto Cleveland's baseball field, where she was tended to by he-who-shall-not-be-thought-of-again if she wanted a record-breaking, championship season.

M. J. changed the channel to *Wheel of Fortune.*

"Can I buy a vowel?" Tanya strolled toward the bar with a cardboard box in hand.

"Totally uninspired," M. J. said, tossing a towel over her shoulder as she picked up two used glasses.

Tanya dropped the box on a stool. "I see you're still in a mood."

M. J. shrugged.

"You know sacks in a scrimmage don't really count toward your sack percentage?"

"I know," M. J. said, swiping the towel across the bar, not at all interested in dissecting her mood or her game play. "What's in the box?"

"Bleach and paper towels. I'm going to help Dad disinfect gear on your doctor's orders."

"He's not my doctor," M. J. snapped.

"Ah. The truth comes out. The shitty mood has nothing to do with those sacks and everything to do with the doctor."

"I hate doctors, remember?" Hopefully M. J. would take the reminder to heart. "And the shitty mood is temporary. I promise."

"Good, then you're allowed to come help me when your shift is over."

"Okay." She could scrub away her frustration.

"But just so you know, since you hate doctors ..." Tanya scrunched her face like she wasn't buying that statement, "one's going to be there."

M. J.'s brows rose along with her heart rate.

"Dad said Dr. Howard is gonna help with the cleaning."

Now she was thoroughly confused. Why wouldn't he call and tell her he was coming over tonight?

"Put on the ball game," a patron yelled.

In that split-second she decided he'd been busy. Busy was good. And going outside of his privileged, suburban comfort zone in order to help people in need was even better.

"Do I detect a smile?" Tanya teased.

"No," M. J. snapped, reminding herself that nothing good—well, aside from that kiss and Dante's medical treatment—came from messing around with Tag.

"Liar. I saw it." Tanya lifted the box. "And hopefully I'll see it later at the gym, too."

By the time M. J. reached the packed gym, a lot of the work was done. Her heart warmed seeing so many people help Pop after he'd helped so many of them. As she moved through the crowd, nodding greetings here and there because the pulsating music was too loud for talking, she looked for Tag. She came upon Tanya on all fours, scrubbing the ring mat instead.

With a poke to Tanya's ass, M. J. got her attention. "Hey," she shouted.

"I told them to turn that down." Tanya was sitting now, leaning close enough so M. J. could hear.

The acridity of the bleach burnt the lining of M. J.'s nose. "Forget turning down the music. Let's get them to open some windows and prop the door."

They did more than that. The few functional fans from last summer were pulled into action, too. It helped. And with the music at a reasonable level, M. J. could finally hear herself think, which wasn't necessarily a good thing, because her first thought was: *Where is he?*

"If you keep looking around like that, your head's going to come unscrewed." Tanya tossed her sponge into the bucket. "He's not here."

"I don't know what you're talking about." M. J. tried to sound sincere and nonchalant, but her brain was already doing the math.

It was after ten. Surely, if Tag was coming, he'd have been here by now.

Tanya slipped beneath the lowest rope of the ring and dropped to the floor. "Can I ask why you just don't call him and see if he's coming?"

"Nope." Because there wasn't an easy answer to that question even though there should be.

Suddenly, a ruckus at the door had her turning toward the sound.

"Wonder what's up?" Tanya asked.

M. J. couldn't hear all the words, but something about "sick wheels" from the kid carrying in an armload of pizzas had her heart slamming in her chest. She jumped to her feet, because she knew it had to be Tag.

Anticipation popped like soda bubbles beneath her skin, tickling her from the inside out, carrying her closer to the door on reluctant feet. She walked toward the crowd, visualizing him coming through the front door, wondering what it would feel like to see him again after that mind-altering kiss.

Pop appeared with grocery bags in hand. Dante followed, hauling more supplies. Mumbles about the car infiltrated her ears along with the nickname *Doc*. Now, she had confirmation, and she was on auto-pilot, closing in on the propped-open front door.

Two large men blocked the entrance, stopping her momentum, giving her a decision to make: step aside and stay put inside the gym, looking like she was waiting for him to come inside, or go outside and greet him, looking like she was eager to see him.

M. J. had never been particularly patient.

Pushing between the men and onto the sidewalk, she told herself she was out here to help carry things. But as she stared at the backside of a BMW with its red taillights disappearing around the corner, a swirl of dread vacuumed up the air in her chest. It had nothing to do with missing out on unloading grocery bags.

M. J. had no idea how long she'd been standing there before she heard Tanya's voice. "Pop said he had something to do."

Staring at the dark street, M. J. nodded.

The whole situation confused the hell out of her, and she couldn't ignore the nagging feeling that said he hadn't called and he didn't stay because he didn't want to see her—probably because, kiss or no kiss, in the light of day, he realized she was too "unorthodox" for him.

All the bravado in the world couldn't erase the pain that came from feeling like she wasn't good enough.

"He's a busy guy," Tanya said.

"Yep, and I'm a busy girl." M. J. tramped the wayward pity-party with the same on-field resolve that let her face down women twice her size in the ultimate battle of strength and will.

There was nothing more between her and Tag than some conversation and a kiss. She wasn't going to let incidental contact compromise her personal code. Not good enough? *Pulleeze.*

M. J. charged into the gym with new purpose. Tomorrow morning she was set to speak at a high school filled with girls who struggled with this very thing. *Not good enough.* She'd be damned if she didn't practice what she preached, and she preached keeping a healthy distance from the people who planted seeds of self-doubt, because that shit grew weeds strong enough to strangle dreams.

If Tag didn't call, fine. If Tag didn't want to see her, that was fine, too. It was better that way. M. J. didn't want to see him, either.

• • •

The next morning, standing in the wings at Maple Side Academy's annual health fair, M. J. got the shock of her life when she saw the man sporting a glossy black business suit and red power tie between the velvet stage curtains.

"Fancy meeting you here." Tag's voice rumbled, low enough to make tiny chill bumps rise on her skin.

Of course, he looked way too good for common sense to remind her of all the reasons she shouldn't be ogling him. Damn that crooked grin.

"Why are you here?" she asked, squeezing sweaty palms together, hoping to hide every last bit of emotion.

"I'm speaking as a last-minute favor. Just a quick address, because I have a … procedure." His face twisted like it had that night at the bar.

Apparently the procedure wasn't something he was looking forward to, and she had the urge to ask if everything was okay. But she kept her lips pressed together, knowing she was already vested enough in this ill-timed, nonsensical acquaintance. Besides, the headmistress had taken the podium and was addressing the all-girl student body.

"I have a special treat for you this year. It is with great pride and pleasure that I introduce my son, Dr. Tag Howard."

M. J. snapped her head around in time to see Dr. Edna Dean step away from the podium with a smile on her face and an arm sweeping toward them.

Tag pressed by M. J. with a palm to her lower back. He didn't say a word as he passed to join *his mother* on-stage, but the heat from his hand remained. M. J. focused on the unnerving sensation as she watched them hug to applause.

Tag was Dr. Dean's son? That was even more unnerving than his physical effect on her body. Edna Dean was one of the most respected women in Cleveland, a truly outspoken advocate for women of all ages, everywhere—and she was Tag's mother. The regal woman walked toward M. J. with a smile on her face. Other than the professional polish and shared emphasis on elite levels of education, M. J. couldn't see a resemblance between her and Tag. Maybe he took after his father.

Edna stood beside M. J., watching her son speak. While M. J. studied the woman's profile in the shadows of the heavy stage curtains, she caught snippets of Tag's speech. Words like disordered eating and female athlete triad caught her attention. If she wasn't so fascinated by his family ties, she'd be hanging on his every word.

"He makes a mother proud," Edna whispered, a wistful smile on her face.

M. J. followed the woman's gaze to the man at the podium. There was no denying he was handsome beyond reason, and smart, too. He flashed that grin, and the student body giggled. M. J. closed her eyes. She was done for. It was hard enough to deny her attraction to him when she thought he was an uptight, social-status minder. But now she knew what she'd suspected all along—there was more to him than what she could see. He was goodhearted, the kind of man who would help out a troubled kid on his own dime, or rearrange his busy schedule to do a favor for his mother.

She opened her eyes when the crowd giggled again.

This was starting to feel like a conspiracy.

Chapter Seven

Tag stood alongside his mother, watching M. J. captivate the crowd of teenage girls. When she spoke, nobody moved, but when she paused at strategic, comedic beats, the laughter was deafening. But the longer Tag listened, the more he questioned the laughter.

M. J. launched into another story from her childhood. This one detailed the time her father and stepmother sent her to summer camp and used the week to buy her a new, more girl-appropriate wardrobe.

"Dresses," M. J. scowled. "Back then, my reaction was this." She stepped away from the podium and stuck her finger into her mouth in a gagging gesture.

The crowd laughed again.

M. J. waited until they settled, to continue. "I cried myself to sleep that first night home, wearing a nightgown with elastic and ruffles that made me itch and literally left indentations in my skin. I cried, because everything I loved was gone. My Jim Brown jersey with a rip in the side where a neighbor kid tried to keep me from rushing into our makeshift end zone. My red, black, and white Air Jordan high-tops that I was wearing when I first touched the rim—jumping off stacked boxes, of course. And so much more. I bawled, because it was like losing a part of me. Those things meant something to me. Those things represented what was important to me. When they threw them away in favor of what they thought was better, it was like they were throwing the real me away, too."

She kept talking, and eventually the audience found something else to be funny, but whatever it was, Tag couldn't laugh. He was stuck on the depressing treatment M. J. had suffered at the hands of her father, and it ignited a familiar burn inside of him.

Tag knew the brutal blow of belittlement firsthand.

Glancing at his watch, he squirmed against the memories pushing to get out, knowing this was only the beginning of the torturous trip down memory lane. In the not-so-distant future, he'd come face to face with his past again. Right about now, Jordon and Grey were on their way to Cleveland. To Tag. For a procedure that could put Grey back in the game. It was an exciting, admirable pursuit. It also made him want to hurl.

If Tag could just keep it professional, he'd be okay.

"She's got them eating out of the palm of her hand. Always," Mom whispered, leaning closer. "Do you know her? I thought maybe her being a football player and you …"

"I do," Tag said, nodding. He knew her well enough to know how she tasted, but he'd had no idea they had something so miserable in common.

But charismatic, self-assured M. J. captivated more than her teenage audience with stories from her depressing youth. She mesmerized Tag, and had him so damn curious. How did she project power and certainty even when she was talking about such horrible things?

God help him, but he wanted—even needed—to know more about her.

"Be a first-rate you, because no matter who you are, that's so much better than being a second-rate whoever they want you to be." Raucous applause and cheers accompanied M. J. as she stepped away from the podium.

The other night, walking along a darkened stretch of sidewalk, he'd likened her to a goddess. Standing before charged-up fans, she was a warrior. He didn't need her protection, but he could use someone who could show him how to rise above the inner turmoil once and for all.

"Fabulous as always," Mom said, grabbing M. J. by the hand as they crossed paths, and then she let go and headed for the podium.

M. J. stopped in front of Tag. He didn't really give her a choice. Unless he moved out of the way, she was surrounded, trapped between walls of rich velvet curtain to her sides, the open stage to her back, and Tag, staring into her shocking-blue eyes.

"Will you have dinner with me?" he asked. "I know you don't date during the season, so we don't have to call it a date. We can call it two friends sharing a meal if it makes you feel better."

She considered him with a blank expression on her face. It was the kind of expression that made a guy never want to open his mouth again. He knew it was a long shot, but if that kiss had imprinted on her brain the way it had on his, there was hope.

"Okay," she said.

His eyes widened. "Tonight?" He might as well capitalize on the unexpected good luck.

She shook her head. "I can't, unless you want to eat at midnight. I have practice and then my shift, but tomorrow I'm free after practice."

At this point, he would take what he could get. "Does six work?"

She nodded again. "But if you tell me to wear a dress, I'll cancel." A little smirk tipped her plump lips, reminding him of how much he wanted to kiss her again.

He leaned closer, brushing her shoulder with his arm as his mouth reached her ear. "What if I ask you to wear those boots?"

"I'd say it was a very odd request coming from a *friend*."

She wasn't buying it either.

"What can I say? I'm an odd guy." She didn't know the half of it.

She smiled. "I can handle wearing them."

He could handle that, too—from her tapered ankles all the way to her strong, shapely thighs. He could even handle more if she wanted him to.

• • •

The thought of M. J. in those boots got Tag through the next twenty-four hours. The grafting procedure wasn't bad thanks to the protective nature of the operating room. Grey was out cold, and Jordon wasn't allowed in, which meant it was easy to keep things professional. Too bad Tag couldn't say the same about the next day's follow-up appointment.

He attempted to keep his distance as he and Leanne checked for meshing in the surrounding tissues, changed the dressings, and informed Jordon and Grey of the progress they could expect to see. But then Leanne got called away. The minute she closed the door behind her, Tag knew his luck had run out.

"How are you?" Jordan asked.

It would've been such a benign question coming from anyone else.

"I'm well." An uncomfortable heat clawed up Tag's face, but he resolved to maintain his composure. "The procedure went well. The hand looks good, and I have every reason to believe this will be a success."

"We're happy to hear that, but that's not what I meant. How are *you*? How have you been? It's …" Jordon's voice cracked, "been a long time."

Tag's jaw ticked as his mind scrambled for a way out of this conversation. *Leave.* But his feet stuck to the floor. Jordon was right; it *had* been a long time. Too long to do anything about it now. "I don't want to talk about this."

Grey's head hung.

"Understood," Jordon said. "So how about I talk and you listen?"

Leave. Tag didn't care who, but someone needed to disappear for this conversation to evaporate, too. Once again, his feet wouldn't cooperate.

"Francis Kemmons was a bastard," Jordon said.

Grey raised his head and grunted his agreement.

"He broke us down with his angry words and volatile behavior. It practically destroyed us all," Jordon said. "It certainly obliterated our bond."

Grey agreed again.

Tag's hands clenched. "Your bond looks fine to me." So much for not talking about this.

"Tag," Jordon stepped closer. "It wasn't always like this. I left home as soon as I could. I left Grey, too, and I didn't call him until a few years ago—after Francis died."

But he didn't call Tag. Twenty-five years, and neither one of his older brothers called to check on him. He stepped back.

"I wanted to call you, too," Jordon continued. "I thought of you off and on over the years, but I was so caught up in my own anger and guilt that I couldn't imagine facing you. I didn't know what I would say. I told myself you were better off without us, and when I looked into it and found out about your medical career, I figured it was true. You were the lucky one. You got away."

It *was* true, but Tag would've felt a hell of a lot luckier had his old life and new life never crossed paths.

"I wish it could've been different, that mom could've lived longer and taken us away from him," Grey said.

The muscles in Tag's jaw tightened. He barely remembered his biological mother, who'd battled cancer off and on for most of his life until she died when he was seven. "I got away," he snapped. "And I'm not going back."

Leanne returned, saving Tag from having to hear more, but the discomfort of a cold sweat remained. Holding all of this in, dealing with the upheaval by himself, was starting to take its toll. If it were any other topic, he'd have talked to his parents by now and asked for their advice, but this was his own private hell, one he didn't want Edna and Simon being subjected to—again. They'd already done so much to get him past those awful, early years, to accept and forget what had happened. He didn't want them to think they'd failed.

He didn't want them to know *he* had.

· · ·

Hours later, sitting in the dirt parking lot in front of Mama Mary's bar and M. J.'s apartment, Tag took a moment to exhale thoughts of Jordon and Grey from his head. He was looking forward to dinner with M. J., and he was not going to let Francis Kemmons ruin another moment in his charmed life. Tag pushed out of the car and spent the next few minutes searching the outside of the crumbling, brick building for an entrance to the apartment upstairs. He'd be lying to himself if he said it didn't bother him that she chose to live here. It might be convenient to work and close to the people she loved, but it didn't seem safe. He wasn't going to bring that up tonight, though. If he did, she'd certainly balk at his concern at best, and label it elitist or sexist at worst. He wasn't interested in taking and defending positions. At this point, he just wanted to have some fun, and M. J. seemed like his best bet.

On his way back around to try the door to the bar, M. J. was standing alongside his car, staring at her phone. Her chestnut hair draped over her shoulders, falling around her face, prompting the overwhelming urge to part the soft curtains so he could cup her face in his hands, rub his thumb over her bottom lip, and kiss her until the heat of the moment melted every last worry from his heart and his head. His heartbeat doubled, priming his body to push her against the car for leverage as he slid a hand over her skin-tight, shiny black pants until he reached the bend in her knee, just above those "ass-kicking" boots. He'd hike that leg to his waist as he deepened the kiss. Heck, after that, he may never have a coherent thought again.

His phone buzzed, and like the good doctor he was he shook off the heady imaginings and pulled it from his dress pants pocket to make sure the call wasn't important.

It was better than important.

It was M. J.

Tag smiled at his screen, and then he smiled at her.

"I was calling to see where you were," she said. "I came out through the bar and you weren't there. I figured you were either down at the gym or dragged off by hoodlums in this scary, urban neighborhood." She faked a shudder and added a sultry laugh.

Tag didn't feel inclined to address the crack about his supposed socioeconomic prejudice, not with her happiness resounding in his ears and her beauty mesmerizing him at close range. "I was looking for you," he said.

"You found me."

"And I'm so glad I did."

Without hesitation, he cupped her face between his hands and pressed her mouth to his, tasting her with his lips and tongue. All the while, he breathed in a warm, clean scent of something earthy, something perfectly suited to M. J., something as legitimate and unpretentious as the woman herself.

Seconds passed. Minutes. He wanted her—needed her—to show him more, teach him more, fill him with so much pleasure he could withstand any pain.

"Uh, I'm leaving now. So if you want to do that, you're welcome to take it upstairs to the apartment."

They separated at the sound of Tanya's voice, their heavy breathing echoing in the stillness.

"Ha, ha," M. J. called out mockingly to her friend as she walked around to the passenger side of Tag's car.

"Hey, Tanya." Tag flashed an extra-bright smile as he followed M. J.

With a hop-like move at the last second possible, he cut in front of her and grabbed the handle. She shot him a lopsided look that questioned his sanity.

"What? I'm opening your car door."

"I know what you're doing. I just don't want you to hurt yourself doing it. Besides, it's unnecessary. This isn't a date, right? And I'm perfectly capable of opening a door by myself."

Not a date. Right. After a kiss like that he wanted to call her bluff.

"Humor me," he said, ushering M. J. into the car with the sweep of his arm.

He couldn't resist touching the small of her back and leaning into the car as she sat. Her lopsided look faded away, replaced by something much more enticing, something that urged him to slip his hand along the seat belt and tug it across her rising and falling breasts.

"I know. I know," he whispered. "It's not a date, and you're perfectly capable of doing this, too, but then I couldn't do this." By the time he said the last word his lips were touching hers.

Before he could do more than initiate the kiss, *his* face was in *her* hands. Their mouths opened, their tongues entwined. The kiss crossed every line of parking-lot propriety ever written. If not for the sound of crunching gravel beneath an approaching car, dinner would've surely been missed.

• • •

If this wasn't a date, then M. J. didn't know what was.

She stole a glance at Tag overtop her menu. The cheesy glow of candlelight flickered across his chiseled face, reflecting off his glasses. *Glasses.* Tiny tingles of pleasure tickled the back of her neck. Who knew glasses on an attractive man really turned her on? The problem was everything about him seemed to turn her on.

"Why don't you wear those all the time?" she asked.

Tag looked at her. "I don't need them all the time. Just to read."

"Aren't you a little young for bifocals?"

A splattering of wrinkles lined his forehead as he reached for his Goose and tonic. She watched him drink, thought about apologizing for the age slight, but decided against it. Either he was being too sensitive or she was being too careful, and neither one would do. If she was going to do this thing, she was going to do it right, without reservations or walking on eggshells whenever he was around.

Tag returned the glass to the table, closed the menu and removed the glasses. "I was born with a congenital cataract. I had surgery years ago. It fixed a lot, but obviously not everything."

The longer he looked at her, the more the muscles in his face relaxed. No more lines on his forehead. No more wrinkles above his nose. Just smooth, flawless skin—skin that she wanted to touch again.

"Put them back on," she said, so softly she didn't recognize her own voice.

"What?" He chuckled.

"You asked me to wear the boots, and I did. Now, I'm asking you to wear the glasses."

Dropping his elbows to the table, he leaned closer, letting the flickering flame from the candle illuminate him. "You like the glasses?"

"I like *you* in the glasses."

He had them on in a flash.

They ordered, and conversation turned to his mother. They'd touched on the topic in the car, talking about the school, the health fair, and the doctor who'd cancelled at the last minute, necessitating Tag's participation, but they never really got into the crazy coincidence of it all.

"Edna Dean is one of my idols," M. J. said, laying her hand over her heart. "I swear. I can't believe she's your mom."

Again, he sipped his drink thoughtfully. "Small world."

"Infinitesimally tiny."

She loved his crooked grin and the way he sort of sucked on his teeth or his tongue—Lord, help her—when he was about to release the grin to speak. "How'd you get involved with Maple Side Academy?"

"Community outreach for the team. We had to fill out a list of things we were passionate about, and I'm passionate about breaking gender barriers and instilling self-worth in young girls. Edna—your mom …" she smiled, because it was just that cool, "called the team and asked if I'd be interested in speaking. I've done it for the past three years."

"You're good at it."

"Thank you." She'd been told that before, but she'd never blushed at anyone else's compliment. She touched fingertips to her heated face. "I enjoy it. Maybe once I retire from football I'll do more of it. Nationwide. I would love that."

Another sip. This time, he tipped the glass until the ice clinked against each side. And then again. He'd done that the night he showed up at the bar, too. The motion filled the silence when he was thinking. He was a doctor. Pondering and studying were probably as common to him as breathing, but sitting there waiting for him to speak again while on the receiving end of his consideration was a little unnerving.

"You don't mind telling hurtful stories like that about your family in public?" he finally asked.

She gathered her thoughts on a drink of her own, letting the cold water dissolve the heat in her chest. "Well, I wish I didn't have those stories to tell, but I do. They make me who I am, and I'm all about owning who I am, so, no. I don't mind."

"Do you talk to them?"

"Who?"

"Your father and stepmother?"

"Too much." M. J. laughed, remembering Felicia's call from earlier today. "A few hours ago, I had a conversation with my stepmom that went something like this. Her: 'Saturday is Annemarie's baby shower.' Me: 'I have a game in Buffalo.' Her: A huge sigh, and then, 'I'll tell them you're sick.' Which is crazy, because everyone knows I play football."

Repeating it made her realize it wasn't really funny that Felicia would rather blatantly lie to people at a baby shower than have to talk about M. J. playing football. But it was what it was, and interactions like that were not going to define her. "I've developed a pretty decent immunity to it all," she said. "Probably *because* I talk about it, and somehow that defuses it."

"Walking away would end it. If you cut ties, then you don't have to deal with it at all."

"Says the man with Edna Dean for a mother. We can't all be so lucky. The rest of us just take what we can get."

With his elbows on the arms of his chair, he steepled his hands in front of his mouth. He bounced his fingertips off his sealed lips enough times to send her in search of something reasonable to say.

When M. J. was about to ask about his father, Tag dropped his hands to the table with a soft thud. "Honestly, I wasn't always that lucky, either. Edna and Simon adopted me."

"Wow."

Okay, that was probably the absolute worst reaction to someone revealing they were adopted. What was the big deal anyway? There wasn't a big deal. But by the pale flush to his face, she could tell either her reaction or the subject was a very big deal to him.

Tag folded his arms across his chest and looked around the restaurant.

"Adoption is a wonderful thing," M. J. said, scrambling to put a positive spin on her reaction. "What's that saying? Adoption is parenthood by choice not chance."

Tag scoffed. "Yeah, well, I'm not sure Edna and Simon would've *chosen* me had they known exactly what I came from."

Again, M. J. had put her booted foot in her mouth. She wished to God she had put it in her ass, instead. A swift kick could've sent them right past this heavy conversation.

So much for a simple lust-filled ruse tonight.

Waiters and waitresses moved around them, refilling glasses, setting down plates. When they finally fluttered away, M. J. picked up her fork and knife and painstakingly cut her filet into bite-sized cubes. She could either take the pause as an opportunity to change the subject and get back to light and easy, or she could push him to confront the uncomfortable, like she would anyone else.

I do not want to be walking on eggshells around anyone, she thought again.

"How old were you when you were adopted?"

His face still wrinkled, but his arms had returned to his sides. "Nine."

"Oh. Well then, surely they would've known your childhood hadn't been easy. They chose you despite what they knew. That's even better."

"They didn't *choose* me. They wanted a child, so they went to social services and specified an age range and checked mild neglect, but no physical or sexual abuse on the forms. They were given me, because I fit the criteria. Of course, they love me now, but I can't help but think if they had the choice between me or, say, a biological child, they'd choose the biological child. I just can't imagine being anyone's first choice." He winced. "You know what? I don't really want to talk about this." An extra-large bite of chicken shoved into his mouth made the statement loud and clear.

That was her cue to back down, wasn't it? She usually missed that sort of thing, and now that she recognized it, she felt guilty not respecting his wishes—even though it bothered her that he had such a negative view on something that clearly worked out for the best. Cue or no cue, she had more to say.

"I disagree. They had the right to refuse the placement in the first place, didn't they? They chose you then. And they chose you again when they made the adoption final. To me, it looks like you were their first choice ... twice."

He blinked at her while he chewed. She'd overstepped his boundaries. He was probably gearing up to throw her out.

"I've never thought of it that way," he said.

She exhaled, and a smile pulled across her face. The gamble had paid off. "A fresh perspective is a good thing."

"It is."

"Edna and Simon sound like good parents."

"They're the best," Tag said without hesitation.

"Then I say they're compensation for whatever happened before them."

Time stilled. She held her breath as he placed his fork on the table and reached out with an open hand, curling his fingers in a way that encouraged her to set her hand in his. When she did, the purest warmth climbed her arm and settled inside her heart.

"You have no idea how badly I needed to hear that." He squeezed her hand. "Thank you."

M. J.'s breathing regulated, and the steady supply of air allowed a satisfied smile to stretch across her face. "You're welcome. And just for the record, despite where you came from, you look like you turned out pretty damn good to me."

He grinned. "You're only saying that because I'm wearing the glasses."

Maybe she was. He was *that* good looking, *that* smooth in those glasses.

Who was this man sitting across from her in a dress shirt so expensive it shined, with not a hair out of place, and eyeglasses sporting a designer label M. J. most certainly couldn't afford on a female quarterback's one hundred dollars per game coupled with a bartender's minimum wage? Who was the scarred boy behind the perfectly coiffed man?

There were numerous warnings in those complicated questions, but as he smiled at her from across the table, heating her entire body with the touch of his hand, M. J. decided some questions were better left unanswered. She liked him, and she couldn't deny that she wanted to be with him. So for now, the only question that seemed important was could she handle seeing Tag during the football season.

She definitely wanted to try.

Chapter Eight

Tag had told M. J. critical things he'd never told anyone, including Edna, Simon, and the parade of therapists from his youth. He'd never confessed his worry that his foster-turned-adoptive parents had bitten off more than they could chew and would've sent him away like his biological father had if they'd known ahead of time the effort it would take to make him into a competent human being. Even after all the hard work and polish, the truth remained written in his genetic code. He'd come from a low-life, mean-spirited, cold-hearted alcoholic, who'd cared more about a stupid sport than he had about his boys. Tag understood biology. He knew some of that could be lurking in him. And tipping others off to that truth didn't sit well with him.

Still, thirty minutes after his revelation, M. J. sat across from him, licking crème brulee off her spoon like nothing he'd said had been a big deal. Maybe it wasn't. Maybe he was skewed. Then again, maybe she didn't particularly care about his family issues, because she had her own. There was power and connection in commiseration like that.

"Do your father and stepmother live in town?" he asked.

She nodded and dipped the spoon in her dessert. "They live in Beachwood."

A sliver of cherry pie stuck in his throat, and he coughed to dislodge it. "*You* are a product of a wealthy suburb?"

"Guilty." She grinned. "My dad's a judge. My stepmom's a retired ballerina, now a committee maven."

Tag would've never guessed. She'd looked so natural, so comfortable in her urban surroundings, and yet she looked pretty damn good sucking on that silver spoon. "Where's your biological mom?"

For the first time all evening, M. J. faltered. Her face flushed as she placed the spoon on the table and stared wistfully into space above his head. He should've known better than to ask a personal question with the potential for causing pain. He wished he'd used more tact or skipped the question all together.

"You don't have to ans—"

"My mom died when I was a baby."

They both spoke at once, and she looked at him them, wincing before a quiet calm settled over her face. "It was in a car accident, so I don't remember her, but I have some pictures, and I've been told stories. She was a high school basketball star. That explains a lot about me, doesn't it?"

Her smile returned, and when it did, Tag marveled at her ability to face the ugly parts of life and push through them with a peaceful outcome. It was inspirational, and it made him want the same for himself. Even more, it made him feel like he owed her something of equal consequence in return for taking the topic down a dark road in the first place.

"My biological mother died when I was seven," he said, pushing through an increasing tightness in his throat.

"Is that why you were put up for adoption, because you were an orphan?"

More tightness. Ruthless tightness. The kind that caused panic to burn his lungs. Tag looked away, thought about changing the subject, thought about running off to the men's room, but when he looked at her, she was staring at him with such earnestness, he knew only a coward wouldn't push on.

"Not exactly," he said. If the waitress had been passing by he would've ordered another drink. "My father was still around. He just didn't want me anymore." *Fuuuuuck.* Tag bit into his left cheek until he tasted blood. It was a welcome distraction from the searing pain in his chest.

M. J.'s pretty face twisted, and she shook her head. Her mouth opened and closed, like her hands, resting on the crisp, white tablecloth. "I'm sorry."

"Don't be."

"But I am. How can I not be? It's a terrible story."

"With a happy ending. Remember, Edna Dean adopted me." Tag tried to smile. It felt funny. He probably looked deranged.

How long would it take for him to accomplish peace like M. J. managed after her moments of upheaval?

"Has he ever tried to contact you? Some biological parents do when they realize they made a mistake."

Tag scowled. "He's dead now. Died in a plane crash a few years ago. And he would've never seen it as a mistake. I sucked at sports. My brothers didn't. He made it clear I didn't belong in baseball, and eventually, I refused to step foot on the field. It was pretty clear-cut as far as a man like Francis Kemmons was concerned. I had to go."

M. J.'s eyes widened. "Kemmons."

Tag wasn't thinking straight anymore. He hadn't been for a long time. Otherwise, he wouldn't have admitted such a guarded thing. And yet, maybe he was just done holding it in. Maybe he needed someone to share the burden. "I take it you recognize the name."

She nodded. "Tanya is a baseball super fan. She has a Fathead of Yadier Molena on the ceiling over her bed … and a Grey Kemmons jersey hanging in her closet."

Tag winced. "Grey is my brother."

"Small world," she whispered.

"Infinitesimally tiny." They were her words from earlier when they'd been talking about his mother, but they applied here, too, and somehow they buoyed him, comforted him with the same connection and shared understanding M. J. effortlessly brought into his life.

She must've recognized the repetition, too, because her mouth curled into the sweetest smile.

It was confusing and surreal that after everything Tag had just admitted, he was happy just being with her.

• • •

M. J. didn't think she'd ever had a meal so fraught with emotional highs and lows outside of dinner at her parents' house, but by the time they'd reached Tag's car, they were laughing.

"I pulled my helmet and skull cap off, and the minute my hair hit my shoulders, the coach started yelling, 'You got burned by a girl,'" she said, continuing with the story she'd started while Tag settled the bill. "Every one of those guys was crying in the handshake line."

She laughed again as she sat, shaking her head, pulling one foot and then the other into the car. That's when she noticed Tag, staring down at her, his laughter gone quiet.

Images from earlier when he'd opened the door, buckled her in, and had his way with her mouth filled her head and heated her face. She wanted him to do it again, and this time, she didn't want him to stop.

He shut the door instead, the crooked smile playing on his lips letting her know he was having similar thoughts. She watched him cross to the driver's side and settle behind the wheel. Just the smell of him in these close quarters had her itching to crawl across the center console. Very unladylike indeed. Why did pushing the boundaries always rev her engines?

"Now where?" he said, his voice wavering the slightest bit.

Maybe she imagined the hesitation. Maybe she wanted vulnerability to be there. Not that he hadn't been vulnerable enough already tonight. Not that she needed him any more exposed. On second thought …

"How about somewhere I can get you naked?"

His laugh sounded like a cough, but he managed to smile.

"You know, if that's all right with you," she added, grinning the entire time.

Tag reached beyond the gearshift and ran his hand along her thigh. "I think I can be good with that."

"You think?" She almost yelped when his fingertips dipped between her legs.

"As long as I can get you naked, too."

M. J. had done it now. She'd let impulse and desire make a decision for her she couldn't possibly refuse—consequences be damned.

With her head against the seat and her eyes closed, she didn't know exactly where they were going when Tag pulled out of the parking lot. It was hard to get caught up in details with his right hand roving her body.

Eventually, she opened the window for air, and as time dragged on, she thought some music would be nice. Then maybe she wouldn't be so self-conscious about her rapid breathing and turned on by his.

He flattened his palm against her belly and dipped fingers beneath the waistband of her pants. How was he managing to stay on the road?

"I hope you don't mind my place," he said. "It was closer."

M. J. opened her eyes as he put two hands on the wheel and pulled into a garage beneath a stately brick townhouse. "I don't mind." And yet she was feeling a little foolish without his wandering hand keeping her thoughts at bay.

Tag exited the car and crossed around the front to her door. A mix of embarrassment and doubt had M. J. frozen, but her arousal lingered. She had suggested this. She wanted this. Him. Complications and all.

"Shall we?" he asked as he opened the door and held out a hand. Such a gentleman.

Still, she paused. *Suck it up, Rooney*, said the coach-like voice in her head. *Nerves are part of every game.* And this was a big one. She hadn't been looking for a man, but she'd found one, and she didn't seem capable of pushing him away. There was something there—even when she didn't want there to be.

M. J. placed her hand in his, because unless she played the game, she'd never find out how it ended.

Tag pulled her through the damp chill of the basement garage and up the stairs behind him. At the top, he let her go, and she stepped into a spotless, sparsely decorated kitchen. Unlike her peeling, sauce-stained laminate countertop, his granite gleamed. No dishes in the sink. Not a bag of bread or chips left open. Perfectly maintained—just like him. Again her worry spiked. But then she remembered he wasn't perfect. Not on the inside. She had the oddest urge to lunge for the cupboards and see what he was hiding in there. More turmoil? M. J. hoped so, because she liked him that way—laid bare. It balanced the playing field.

She faced him as he shut the basement door. "I wish I had known you then."

"When?" He reached up with one hand and loosened his tie.

"When you were a boy."

Her answer startled him into stopping mid-motion, leaving the tie hitched around his neck like a designer noose. "Why?"

She walked to him and finished the job, slipping the tie over his head. "Because we would've been quite the pair, don't you think?" She smoothed her hands over his shoulders and up to his neck. "You, the boy who felt unloved because he refused to get on the field, and me, the girl who felt unloved because she refused to get off it."

His warm hands slid over the curves of her ass to the small of her back, urging her closer. "The way you see things blows my mind."

"We can find better things to blow."

Eyes wide, mouth open, and head tipped back, he laughed. It was the most beautiful sound M. J. had ever heard. Placing her lips against the vibration in his throat, she quieted him. He smelled like mulled spice and tasted like salted bread—pure comfort. Lust zip-lined from her heart to the hot spring between her legs.

He cupped her jaw, tilted her head, and covered her mouth with his. Gentle suction, warm and wet, so soft and unassuming she didn't realize how far gone she was until her head was spinning from lack of air.

"The bedroom's upstairs." He stared down at her with cloudy eyes, raking his fingers through the hair on the sides of her head, lulling her into the sweetest surrender.

M. J. didn't care where they went. She was more than fine right here, but she followed him up another flight of stairs, her heart swelling with every step. What was it about this man that made her feel strong when she was being weak?

He pulled her into the first room on the right, wrapping her in his arms. "For the record, when I was on the field with you, I didn't mind being there at all."

"When I fell?"

He nodded.

M. J. felt suddenly sad their first meeting was one-sided. "I'm sorry I don't remember that."

"Funny, I don't think I'll ever forget it."

He kissed her, slow and deep, until the heat at the core of her body melted everything in its path, buckling her knees. She curled her hands into his shirt to keep from slipping to the ground.

Blackout curtains and no light from the hall meant the room was dark, and M. J. had no idea the direction of the bed. She needed the bed. Her legs were not going to hold out. Some professional athlete she turned out to be. Where was her almighty stamina now? Busy, trying to keep pace with her pounding heart, because Tag traced the length of her neck with his fingertips, and then his lips followed.

He tugged the shirt from her shoulder and licked her there, causing her to sway. She had no choice but to curl her hands around the waistband of his pants for balance.

"Come here," he growled, pulling her deeper into the darkness.

Finally a bed. She hit it hard, falling and bringing him down on top of her.

More kisses mixed with groping and heavy breathing through open mouths. Every inch of her skin burned. She pressed her shoulder blades into the mattress, arching her back, pushing her breasts toward him. He took the not-so-subtle hint, lifting her shirt, skimming her belly with his hand and flicking a thumb across her aching nipple until she moaned against his mouth.

He did it over and over again.

Somehow, in the midst of it all, M. J. managed to free enough buttons on his shirt to pull it over his head. She grazed the flexing muscles of his shoulders and back on her way to his ass. He felt so good, every part of him soft over hard.

Piece by piece, more clothing vanished, until they were bare, and every inch was explored in every position imaginable. There hadn't been a workout in her entire athletic career that left her this physically and mentally drained.

And they weren't done yet. Not even close.

• • •

With his arms wrapped around her, Tag rolled until he was flat on his back. They'd been jockeying for some kind of leadership position since this marathon began. He figured it was time somebody just rolled over and surrendered. With her straddling him, running soft, strong hands over the core of his body, he didn't mind one bit that the somebody was him.

He reached up and held her breasts in his hands, loving the way she hissed an exhaling breath when he teased. He skimmed her ribcage and her waist, releasing a hiss of his own when she palmed his erection to slide on the condom. And then his fingers were smoothing up and down the slippery heat between her overstretched legs. Her moans vibrated through him, creating a synergy he'd never experienced.

With control fading fast, Tag gripped her hips and entered. Pleasure poured over him, warming him from the inside out, causing a fuzzy high in his head. He watched as she moved, nothing more than a shadow above him. He kept hands roving her body to remember she was real.

As the pace quickened, so did their breathing, until the fuzzy high felt like impending unconsciousness. Tag broke first with a guttural sound rising from his throat. She leaned forward, her weight on her hands, rubbing against him until she shuddered too.

Spent did not begin to describe the feeling.

Several labored breaths later, she whispered in his ear, "That was so good."

"Too good," he chuckled. "I think you ruined me."

"Then I'll have to fix you." She smoothed kisses over his jaw to his lips.

He felt so full, so right; maybe she already did.

Chapter Nine

Whoever said things looked better in the morning was wrong. As far as M. J. was concerned, where there was sunlight, there was panic.

She stared at the open bedroom door and the brightening hallway. Being in Tag's bed felt wrong, and not because of the sex. The sex had felt all sorts of right, like a full game of perfectly executed plays. But being here when the sun came up carried expectations.

M. J. had never been any good at meeting off-field expectations.

Slipping out of bed, she picked her clothes off the floor and wandered the hall in search of the bath. After she dressed and faced her reflection, she returned to the bedroom, standing in the doorway, watching him sleep. It was still too dark to see details, but she could hear his even breathing. He was so peaceful. And why shouldn't he be? He'd had one hell of a night.

M. J. smiled and considered crawling back into bed with him. After all, she'd had one hell of a night, too. But she couldn't shake the feeling that things would turn uncomfortable when he woke. Maybe he'd want more than she could give. At this point, she had nothing more to offer.

She glanced at the glowing bedside clock, conscious of the fact she had an away game this weekend. The bus would be leaving at noon. It was yet another reason she didn't belong in that bed. Her focus needed to be on Buffalo's brick-wall defense, not Tag.

Pushing off the jamb, she decided once and for all to let him sleep. In the kitchen, she dialed her phone and used an unopened piece of mail to provide Tanya with Tag's address, and then M. J. scribbled a note on the envelope's blank backside.

I had to get ready for my game. Thanks for last night.

M. J.

Sitting in the passenger seat of Tanya's car, two blocks away from Tag's, M. J. realized exactly where she was—less than a mile away from her parents' house.

"Uncanny, isn't it?" Tanya asked.

"More like unsettling."

"Do you want to stop and say hello? Maybe have a croissant?" Tanya mangled the word on purpose.

"Hell, no." M. J. said emphatically even though she knew Tanya was teasing. "Although, they'd probably let the whole walk-of-shame thing slide if they knew he was a doctor. They'd think it meant there was hope for Maya Jane yet."

"Considering your shirt's on inside out and your bra strap is hanging from your handbag, I doubt that."

M. J. laughed. The sound scattered some of the heaviness from her head.

"Are you going to see him again?"

M. J. quieted. "I don't know."

"Let me rephrase that: do you want to see him again?"

"I don't know."

"That bad?"

"That *good*," she whispered. From the dinner, to the conversation, to the sex. "But you know me. I just can't figure out how I'd fit with that kind of man. In Beechwood. A quick jog from the parents. It makes me wonder at what point he'll *realize* I don't fit and try to change me." She cringed.

"Maybe he won't try to change you."

"Maybe." It was all so complicated—too complicated. Men like Coach and Pop, who really, truly understood a woman like M. J., were rare. "I don't want to talk about it or think about it anymore. I want to focus on Buffalo. Football first." Because that was the more important thing.

If M. J. wanted to be a legitimate champion, it couldn't be any other way.

• • •

Tag reached an arm across the empty side of his bed. He wasn't exactly surprised she wasn't there. The last thing she'd said before she drifted off to sleep was that she was breaking the rules by being here. Something about warriors and sex before battle. He found it cute and a nod to his skills of persuasion. And yet, now she was gone, and he was disappointed he hadn't been more convincing.

There was no rhyme or reason to his thoughts as he pushed out of bed and padded to the shower. Who picked her up to take her home? Probably Tanya. Unless she called a cab. He didn't like the idea of her spending money on a car when he had a perfectly operational one in the garage. Last night, when he'd pulled into that garage with her sitting flushed by his side, there'd been so much anticipation. They'd been good together, good enough she should've stayed for a morning kiss.

Halfway through his shower, Tag decided he wanted more from her. For starters, he wanted to see her again. Dinner. Lunch. Breakfast. Whatever she'd agree to. But that was the problem. He had no idea what she wanted now that she'd left without the benefit of some coffee and conversation to determine what last night meant.

Out of the shower and dressed for a run, Tag headed downstairs to the kitchen where he'd left his cell phone on the counter next to his keys. He found a note scribbled on a business envelope. It wasn't much of a note. Two lines lacking any revealing adjectives, followed by two letters. But M. J. was like that—to the point. *Someplace where I can get you naked.* Finally, he smiled.

Snatching his phone off the counter, he opened a new text message, addressing it to her and typing, *Good luck in Buffalo.*

That was where her focus needed to be at the moment, not on explaining to him why she bailed from his bed. If things worked out the way he wanted them to, he'd have plenty of time to get the answer to that—and then make sure it didn't happen again.

Tag's elevated mood lasted through a five-mile run fueled with memories from last night. Only when he returned home and checked his phone to find M. J. hadn't replied to his text with so much as a *thanks* did his mood begin to sink.

He couldn't seem to find his footing after that.

As he moved through a lighter than usual Friday, thoughts of M. J. lurked in his mind, ready to pounce whenever he wasn't preoccupied with medicine. How hard was it to text back? He checked his phone obsessively. Maybe she didn't get his text? He composed several follow-ups only to delete them before he hit *send*. Maybe she was just that focused on her game?

By Saturday afternoon, he craved some connection to her, so he passed on lunch with his parents in order to listen to the web broadcast of the Clash game. They lost, with M. J. fumbling and throwing a pick-six. He had a sinking feeling he wouldn't hear from her for a while now.

Professional athletes hated losing, which made Tag think about Grey. Monday was another follow-up appointment, and Tag was anxious to check the progress on the wound. A nagging heaviness in his chest told him he was in for more personal talk with Jordon and Grey. He only hoped he could handle the conversation half as well as he handled the subject matter while at dinner with M. J.

Monday arrived, dark and dreary with a few rumbles of thunder. The weather was fitting. Tag took a deep breath and held it in his lungs while he stood outside the exam room. On the exhale, he told himself he was capable of handling whatever happened.

Following the exam, which revealed impressive progress, a clearly exhilarated Grey gripped Tag's hand. There was strength in the right-handed motion, and at first, Tag thought it nothing more than a display of his capabilities since the procedure. But then, Grey didn't let go.

"I didn't say much the other day, but I wanted to say it now—before I lost my chance. I am so fucking sorry, man. I was a fool. I let him be a big part of my life for way too long, even after I learned he'd stolen Jordon's signing bonus, right up until he left the country with my girl. I was so stupid! I meant it when I said I wished things could be different. You and Jordon should've been part of my life all those years, not him."

Thick sadness blocked air to Tag's lungs, and he nodded, because it seemed like the right thing to do. He'd never figured his father had screwed over his "meal tickets," too.

Jordon pulled the phone from his pocket. "I want to show you something."

The gaping hole in Tag's gut had him thinking it was something he didn't want to see, but he didn't have a choice. Jordon shoved the phone in front of Tag's face, showing off a smiling baby boy wearing a Nashville Argonauts baseball cap.

"You have a nephew." Jordon slapped Tag's back. "My son. His name's Braydon."

Tag blinked a few times. "Congratulations," he said, unable to wrap his already-reeling mind around the revelation. He was more than a brother now; he was an uncle. He latched his watery gaze onto Grey's healing hand. "We'll start the countdown now. Two more months, then you can start rigorous rehab. If all goes well, you'll be in Tampa for spring training."

Jordon and Grey seemingly took the hint, accepting the sudden subject change. More thanks for Grey's progress resounded, no more apologies or talk about nephews. But when they'd gone, Tag caught himself wondering. Was Grey married too? Did he have kids? Did Jordon's family and Grey's family get together for holidays and summer vacations?

An odd sort of longing pulled at Tag's heart, but he was too emotionally beaten to process any of it. The good news was, barring any complications, he didn't have to see Jordon and Grey ever again.

Maybe now that he had, he could start to heal.

• • •

"So you're really not going to see him again?" Tanya tightened her boxing gloves.

It wasn't the first time she'd asked since picking M. J. up from Tag's, but M. J. had forbidden it as a topic of conversation anywhere near the football field. Apparently she needed to forbid it at the gym, too, so that a good, hard workout could be had.

"No," M. J. said as she tugged her headgear into place. "I'm not going to seek him out until maybe after the season ends."

Tanya slammed her padded fists together. "Don't you think you should tell him that?"

"Contact will distract me. I can't have anything distracting me. You saw what happens when I'm distracted."

Her performance versus Buffalo had been an embarrassment. Had she spent the night before that game in her own bed with her thoughts firmly focused on football, things would've turned out differently.

"M. J., Buffalo is a good team."

"We are a better team, and we would've won that game had I been firing on all cylinders." She grabbed her gloves off the bench and headed for the ring. "But if it makes you stop talking about it, I'll text him." After all, one could argue it had been rude and cowardly to leave him hanging this long. "I'll tell him I made a mistake, and it's not going to happen again. I can't be seeing anyone during the season, which is what I tried to tell him in the first place."

Too bad it hadn't stopped *her* from propositioning *him*.

M. J. agonized over what to text, and in the end, she wanted to take it back the minute the message was sent. She should've stuck to her guns and simply avoided him. The *thanks for the evening, but we can't do it again* text was supposed to absolve her of her guilt over the way she'd left and her lack of contact with him, but it sort of backfired. His lack of response gave her something new to deliberate. Maybe he didn't even care.

By midweek, M. J. was annoyed by everything.

"Franks, what the fuck was that?" she got in her tight end's face, mask to mask. "You weren't supposed to drift until you made contact with me."

"I made a mistake."

"Don't make one again."

Tanya wedged them apart with her hands. "Settle."

"Ladies," Coach bellowed.

M. J. snatched a water bottle from the carrier and squirted a stream into her mouth.

"What's your problem?" Tanya asked.

"My problem? People who aren't where they're fucking supposed to be so they can catch a pass. That's my problem."

"Bullshit. You've been off all week. This about you-know-who? Thought you were done with all that?"

Coach bellowed again. "Can we run a successful play sometime before sunset?"

It seemed like everyone was looking at M. J.

She dropped the water bottle into its slot and lifted her face to the bright blue sky. She was being a complete idiot. "I'm sorry," she said.

Better yet, she proved it by executing five flawless plays to bring practice to an early end. In that moment, she felt like herself again.

Saturday rolled around with M. J. settled and focused. Nothing mattered but what happened on the field. It was easy to keep the momentum going when they were up by three touchdowns come halftime. And M. J. felt downright indestructible when she added three more passing touchdowns in the second half.

Buffalo was a distant memory as she showered and dressed. She was clearly capable of taking control after upheaval and righting a sinking ship.

"Are you coming with us?" Tanya asked over the noise of celebration and hairdryers. "We're going to shoot some pool."

M. J. nodded. "Heck, yeah." A night out with her team was just what she needed to solidify her return to gridiron glory.

She tied her damp hair into a knot at the base of her neck and tidied up her locker before heading down the hallway to the exit. As she walked, she pulled her phone from her purse and checked messages. There wasn't so much as a missed call.

Some of her exuberance waned.

She stared at the list of undeleted text messages, zeroing in on her last interaction with Tag, but this fresh disappointment wasn't about him.

Clicking on the message at the top of the list, she typed, "We won. 42-10. Four passing TDs. 150-yard game," and sent the words to Dad. She sent a similar text after every game, wanting him to know in case someday he decided to care.

As she pushed through the fieldhouse door, knowing she'd come face-to-face with Tanya's adoring family, she wondered what it would feel like to have her family waiting instead, not that she'd ever have that many people waiting for her. She was an only child after all.

In a brush of luck, the general area outside the locker room was empty except for the referees engaged in some post-game conversation ... and Tag. He stood off to the side in a spot overshadowed by a soda machine, wearing khaki shorts, hooded sweatshirt, and uncharacteristically messy hair.

She would've missed him if her body hadn't reacted like a virtual magnet to his.

"I'm sorry. I couldn't stay away," he said when she stopped in front of him.

"That's okay." In a completely contradictory way to how she'd been feeling for most of the week, she liked the idea of him being here, seeing her win.

At least someone had.

"You're amazing." He shoved a hand through his hair. "That thirty-yarder?" He whistled. "On a rope!"

"Thank you." She smiled, taking in his disheveled appearance again. "You're a mess."

He nodded, adding a self-deprecating chuckle. "I know. It's … I've had better weeks."

"Because of me?"

"That didn't help." A small smile curled his beautiful lips, bringing her gaze to his mouth, where her memories turned intimate. "But honestly, I've been thinking a lot about my brothers." He exhaled. "I saw them."

"Rooney, you coming?" one of her teammates yelled.

A few other people, strangers, milled around. This did not seem like an appropriate place to be having a heavy conversation.

M. J. held up a finger over her head, signaling to her teammates that she'd be there in a minute, and then she stepped closer to Tag.

"I'm sorry," he said. "You should go. I shouldn't be bothering you. Really, I just wanted to see you play. It's a nice diversion." He smiled again, but he still managed to look so damn sad.

"Let's go, Rooney."

"I'll drive myself," she called over her shoulder.

"Go," he said.

How could she leave him like this?

"Come with us," she said, wondering why in the hell she actually said it.

"You don't mean that."

She wasn't sure that even mattered, now that she'd offered. It wasn't like she could add to his torment by taking the invitation back. Besides, it didn't feel right for her to be so happy while he was so sad.

"We can talk in the car on our way," she said. "And then you can loosen up a little bit, because you look like you need it. Believe me, there will be no shortage of fun with this crew following a win like that."

She just hoped she could remain in control and impartial enough to not let things go too far again.

Chapter Ten

Tag drank a draught while he watched M. J. bend over a pool table. He couldn't think of a better way to spend an evening.

She knew about Grey's hand, now, and Jordon's son, too. After the car ride here, she knew everything … except that knowing those things made her indispensable to Tag. He couldn't imagine not having her to talk to. She balanced out the extremes.

Again he wanted more from her, much more than her last text allowed, which was nothing until her season ended. But she'd asked him to be here, and it gave him hope.

"Doc, you want next game?" Tanya was holding the butt end of a cue stick toward him.

Maybe it was the beer. Maybe it was the way M. J. smiled at him with her hip perched against the table. Whatever the reason, a man who avoided competitive games like the swine flu, grabbed hold of the stick and accepted the challenge.

"Do you play?" M. J. asked, glancing at him through a flutter of thick lashes as she packed balls into the triangle.

"Never," he said, smiling.

"Oh, you poor, poor, man."

"I take it you play a lot."

She moved around the end of the table. "Nah, I'm just generally good at everything."

She sunk four balls on the initial break.

Tag only had one chance to shoot. He failed miserably, sending the ball on a crooked path into the padded side. After that, he was relegated to watching M. J.

There were worse things to do.

He bore no hard feelings over the decisive loss, especially when she sunk the final ball and sauntered toward him to retrieve his cue. Their hands brushed as the stick transferred between them.

"Impressive win," he said, feeling the desire build inside of him.

She nodded, and her soft smile erased. "I'm sorry. Maybe I should've let you win, considering the week you've had." Her expression and words were serious, but the whole idea that she was considering placating him with a thrown pool game was enough to make him laugh.

She must've caught on to the absurdity, because she laughed, too. The sound brought his desire to the overflow point, and the sparkle in her eyes threatened to ignite him.

If she was in the mood to soothe him, he had a better idea.

"I want you to come home with me." He slipped a hand to her waist and pulled her closer.

Surprisingly, there was no resistance. Their thighs met before her lips touched his, but then she pulled back, a few lines of concern on her beautiful face. "I don't know about that."

It wasn't perfect, but it was much better than *no*.

An hour later, Tag was buying rounds for most of the team. A few, like M. J. and Tanya, refused to drink a drop of alcohol during the season, but they joined in by chanting and teasing. A couple times, M. J.'s hand smoothed across his back as he sat on the end stool and she stood behind him. It always seemed to coincide with her leaning forward to refill her water glass, but it still felt good to be close to her. It felt good to be close to all of them. Loud, lively, a few of them vulgar, such a change from the quiet, calculation he'd orchestrated for his life.

These days, the only thing quiet calculation gave him was extra time to contemplate his next step—if any—as far as Jordon and Grey were concerned.

"I bet Doc knows what this scar is. You know?" one of the players asked as she hiked up the sleeve of her blouse and shoved her elbow toward him.

A long white line of thick, traumatized skin graced the inside of her elbow. Mesmerized, Tag leaned closer and lifted his hand. "May I," he asked before touching her and bringing the arm closer for inspection. "Tommy John surgery."

"Bingo. When I was fourteen. I played a lot of softball."

"How about this one?" someone else asked.

The next ten minutes were a veritable flash of scarred flesh from the women around the bar. Two knee surgeries, an Achilles repair, and a labral tear. He was rather enjoying himself, always eager to talk medicine, and professional athletes—men or women—were all the same, eager to talk injuries.

"I've got you all beat," M. J. said, working her way between his legs. His gut cramped as she lifted the hem of her shirt until he could see the lace of her bra. "Guess how I got this?"

There were some moans of concession in the distance, but it was hard to know who they were coming from with his heartbeat echoing in his head.

An inch-wide scar marred the taunt skin just below the curve of her breast. He ran a finger over it, feeling her muscles contract. "Surgical tube site?" he questioned. He honestly wasn't sure. The heat from her body had him struggling to speak, let alone think.

"Wrong," she whispered. "Speared with a broken hockey stick."

"Damn." He flattened his palm against her stomach and slid it to her waist, brushing his thumb over the injury site. "How long ago?"

"Senior year of high school." She looked down at the spot where his hand remained. "I thought about getting a tattoo to cover it up, but honestly, I kind of like it now. It's a good conversation starter."

She was the strangest, most amazing woman he'd ever met.

Somewhere along the line, everyone else had redistributed their attention, leaving them alone at the end of the bar. "Come home with me," Tag said again.

She shook her head, but one more brush of his thumb over her abdomen, and she smiled. "Okay."

•••

How bad would it be to sleep with him again after one abysmal game she attributed indirectly to the night she spent with him? She'd told him twice she couldn't see him during the season, and here she was again—seeing him. How weak was that? *Weak.* But apparently she was also now too weak to care, because she was back in his house, and she knew she would be the minute she'd seen her teammates tempting him with some warped version of sports-medicine porn. She was too competitive for her own good.

But it was more than that. What started out as genuine concern for the disheveled man standing outside the locker room turned into something less complicated during the course of the evening. It seemed like such a shame to not explore this resilient thing between them.

"Sorry," he said, as he tossed his cell phone on the coffee table and settled beside her on the couch. "There's no true on-call in sports medicine, but there's always somebody getting hurt and wanting answers."

M. J. wanted answers, too, like what would happen next, and was it possible for her to compartmentalize her life enough to have both a winning football season and a successful relationship? She didn't get a chance to ask the question, because his phone rang again.

They simultaneously glanced at the vibrating object, and then made eye contact.

Jordon Kemmons flashed on the screen.

Tag didn't make a move toward the phone.

"Are you going to answer it?" M. J. asked.

He shook his head.

M. J. reached up and circled her fingers in the tight cords of his neck. "Do you want to talk about it?"

He looked at her with darkened eyes. "I don't want to talk about anything." His hand returned to her leg, sliding up her thigh as his body twisted toward her.

She met his mouth halfway, letting her lips say what her brain couldn't seem to piece together moments ago. She wanted to make him feel better. If only for the time being, she wanted to help him forget.

Lifting the shirt over his back as their mouths intertwined, M. J. maneuvered until she straddled him. With a flick of her wrist, she tossed the T-shirt to the floor and smoothed her hands over his sculpted chest. He returned the favor, ridding her of her blouse, her bra, touching her with wide-eyed reverence.

Too much energy trapped in her chest cavity, pushing against her lungs, making her breaths short and wheezy.

"When I wake up tomorrow morning, I want you to be there," he said.

At the moment, she wanted to be there, too. She wanted to manage both a man and a football career. It was something she'd never wanted before, because there'd never been anyone worth the risk.

This man was a game changer. And after today's game, she believed in her capabilities far too much to not give this a second chance.

• • •

Tag wasn't alone when he woke. As he watched M. J. sleeping, facing him, hand curled beneath her chin, a sliver of brown hair fluttered in the soft exhales from her nose. How was it possible for one person to contain so many different parts? The brash and aggression of an athlete, the wit and caring of a woman, and the innocence of a child in her sleep. All parts combined to create someone fascinating, someone who proved he'd been striving for one-dimensional far too long.

He stayed there, admiring her in the faint traces of morning sun, wondering how it was even possible a woman like M. J. wanted anything to do with him. Tag winced, because he recognized the hang-up. Underneath all the success, Francis Kemmons's discarded son never thought he was good enough for anyone, and it was getting old. *Finally.*

His phone buzzed, and M. J. stirred. Slipping out of bed, he pulled on his boxers and grabbed the phone off the clock where it had been charging. Not until he was in the hallway did he glance at the screen. *Grey.*

Considering Tag had ignored Jordon's call last night, maybe he should answer Grey's call this morning. Maybe the hand wound had opened again.

"Hello," Tag said as he walked downstairs.

"Hey." The ensuing silence was more confusing than unnerving.

"How's the hand?"

"Oh, fine. Great, actually."

"Good." So why was he calling? Was he calling to *chat*? Tag leaned against the kitchen counter, scrubbing the sleep from his eyes.

"Listen, this is lame. I'm trying not to make it lame, but it's not easy, and well … I wanted to call and ask you something. Jordon and his family are here until tomorrow evening. I thought this could be our only shot at, you know, getting all of us together. Would you come for a visit?"

Pittsburgh was a couple hours from Cleveland, an easy day trip, but not so easy when a questionable family reunion was on the other end.

Reasons why Tag couldn't—shouldn't—started lining up in his head until he remembered what he'd told himself before he'd climbed out of bed: the familial hang-ups were getting old. It was time to move on. Was this the way to once and for all put the demons to rest?

"Nel, my fiancée, is a great cook, so we promise to feed you well, and Braydon is guaranteed to make you laugh. Between him and my dogs, I don't know who gets into more trouble." Grey quieted. "Am I trying too hard?"

Apparently Tag wasn't the only self-conscious Kemmons brother. "No," he said, feeling his resistance melt to a more comfortable level. He sat in the nearest chair. "I don't think I've been trying hard enough."

The exhale on the other end of the phone sounded a lot like relief. "So you'll come?"

"He'll come?" a faint, female voice repeated on Grey's end of the line.

Grey shushed whoever it was.

This was a group effort? The thought prompted an awkward smile. "I'll come." But he wasn't at all certain he'd have the guts to actually get there.

Tag was sitting on the edge of the bed, staring at unopened emails, when M. J. woke. She crawled toward him and pressed a kiss to the back of his neck.

"I'm still here," she whispered.

Warmth flooded him, temporarily overriding his anxiousness about the day's plans. He kissed her forehead. "You have no idea how thankful I am for that."

"You could show me," she said, smoothing her hands beneath his shirt and over his stomach.

"Oh, I will, but I need to ask you something first."

She stilled. "What?"

"Will you drive to Pittsburgh with me today to hang out with my brothers?"

He knew Sunday was her only day off from practice and bartending. He was asking a lot for her to spend it with him. "I really don't want to go alone, and you're the only person who knows this whole sordid story."

She wrapped her arms around his neck and pulled him to the mattress. "I'd be honored to."

Four hours later, they were showered, dressed, and he was surprisingly calm as he followed the last directive from his GPS.

M. J. reached out and covered his hand, resting on the gear shift. When he glanced at her, she smiled, a quiet show of support, an instant accelerant for his mood. He smiled back, flipping his hand so he could hold hers. He had to believe her being here made all the difference. He couldn't imagine making this trip alone.

"How are you going to introduce me?" she asked.

His smile widened. "M. J. Rooney and her rocket for an arm."

She laughed. "That's not bad."

The air stilled, and seriousness settled over them. "How do you want me to introduce you?"

They were still holding hands, and he liked the warmth and solidarity in the union. It'd been a long time since he felt like a part of something intimate like this.

"You can use whatever you're comfortable with."

But neither one of them looked particularly comfortable. M. J. crossed and uncrossed her legs in the narrow space beneath the dashboard, and Tag's palms began to sweat. He gripped the wheel with both hands and considered introducing her as his friend, but she was more than that, and he wanted more than that.

"Can we say we're dating yet?" Thank God he was driving, because he wasn't sure he wanted to see her reaction.

"I'd say that's the least of what we're doing."

He looked then, probably portraying more shock than he wanted to. He felt like he was seventeen again. "So what are you saying?"

"We're dating." She laughed. "And that should help me get you naked more often."

"Trust me. You don't need help with that."

They held hands as they walked up to Grey's front door. It helped stabilize Tag's churning stomach. But the minute M. J. pressed the doorbell, reality hit like a rug pulled out from beneath his feet.

This wasn't some leisurely Sunday drive with the fascinating woman he was dating. This was the first step in healing the hurt from his past. Tag wasn't sure he'd given that part enough thought.

But it was too late.

The door swung open, revealing Grey. "Man, I'm so damn glad you came."

What followed was an awkward hug-like greeting, as Grey pulled him into the foyer. "Is this your girl?" he asked, smiling at M. J.

Tag nodded. "This is M. J. Rooney."

M. J. smiled back and shook Grey's hand. "Nice to meet you."

"I put the dogs in the den," said a petite blonde, striding toward them. "Braydon is none-to-happy, but I figured our guests could use some downtime after the drive. Nel Parker," she said, reaching a hand toward Tag. "You've got Grey's eyes. It's so nice to finally meet you. Thank you for everything you've done to get him back on the field."

"I'm not there yet, babe."

Tag glanced at his brother who was gripping the woman by the shoulders, rubbing affectionately. The hand looked good. As much as Tag wanted to take solace in medical concerns, he'd wait to take a closer look at the hand until the introductions were complete. "It's nice to meet you, too," Tag said.

"This is Tag's girl, M. J.," Grey said.

It sounded surreal, but it felt right, too.

After the women exchanged handshakes, Nel waved them deeper into the room. "Maggie is feeding Braydon. Jordon is on a call. Enjoy the calm before the storm." She shared a look and a laugh with Grey. "Can I get you something to drink? Beer, wine, margarita? We have some left from last night."

"Beer sounds good," Tag said. It was something to quench his thirst and eradicate the small buzz of nerves. So far, things had been easy, maybe too easy. Certainly the pleasantries couldn't last. Sooner or later, someone was bound to say something that dredged up old memories, halting this effortless forward progress.

"I'll have water," M. J. said.

"Are you sure?" Nel asked.

"No alcohol in season." Tag reached for M. J.'s hand on a burst of protective pride. "M. J. plays quarterback for the Cleveland Clash."

"You'll fit right in." The booming voice preceded the imposing man. Jordon emerged from the shadowed hall and extended a hand to M. J. "Sports are the Kemmons family religion."

Tag watched the greeting, knowing Jordon hadn't meant any slight by the words. He felt it, too, when Jordon offered him a hearty welcome. But a little nugget of doubt and separation had been planted with that innocent statement. *Sports are the Kemmons family religion.*

Tag didn't play sports, so what did that make him? "Not a Kemmons," his biological father would've said.

Tag had driven two hours on a Sunday afternoon, hoping to quiet that voice in his head. He only hoped he didn't end up back in Cleveland with the voice louder than ever.

Chapter Eleven

M. J. sat beside Tag at a dinner table surrounded by interesting, accommodating strangers in a house bigger and more beautiful than anything her parents had. To call today surreal would be an understatement.

"Asparagus?" Tag asked as he held a floral-patterned plate.

He was nervous. She could tell. The lopsided grin hadn't appeared since Jordon had made an entrance. Jordon *was* daunting, but M. J. suspected there was more to it than that. After all, if she thought the day was unreal, Tag must be reeling. He was having dinner with his biological family, sitting alongside "his girl."

She smiled as she accepted the platter and scooped a serving onto her plate. They were officially dating. She'd said it was okay, but the idea bounced around her brain like a caged rabbit. Hopefully she'd get used to it, and it would settle. After all, she was sleeping with him and meeting his family. Dating seemed like a minimum requirement for those things.

She stuffed an oversized piece of lasagna into her mouth. It was a lot to swallow, but she was not going to make this day about her in-season relationship hang-ups.

"So Tag, may I ask where you get the … materials to perform a procedure like what Grey had done?" Jordon's wife, Maggie, asked. She had the baby pressed to her chest in some sling-like contraption. The kid was non-stop smiley, and one of the cutest things M. J. had ever seen.

"No, you may not," Jordon said.

How something so smiley came from something so stern was beyond her.

Maggie shot him a side-eyed glance, and then smiled at Tag. "Is it humane?"

Prior to sitting down to dinner, they'd all been briefed on herbivore vs. carnivore dishes. It seemed to be more than a choice Maggie made to keep her rail-thin figure.

"'Is it effective?' is my preferred question," Jordon said in his same gruff manner, but then he leaned over and kissed his wife on the ball of her rosy cheek.

"We have the answer, and it's, 'Yes.'" Grey lifted his hand and gave a beauty-queen-like wave.

M. J. liked the way Nel smiled at him, all glistening eyes and proud.

A spark tingled in M. J.'s chest when she looked at Tag. "He's a great doctor." The spark exploded when he smiled back, and a warm hand landed on her thigh beneath the table.

"How did you guys meet?" Maggie asked.

Braydon squealed as he gnawed on the fabric closest to his mouth.

Tag squeezed M. J.'s leg. "Technically, she doesn't remember how we met, because she had a concussion."

"A sack?" Grey asked.

"Uh, no. I fell onto the field at a baseball game he was covering."

They laughed. Tag filled them in on the rest of the story with an easy divulgence. If she didn't know the story behind the smiles around the table, she'd have thought this a routine family dinner.

Placing a hand on top of Tag's, M. J. reminded herself it was anything but. Still, she hoped these people were as transparent as they seemed. No hidden agendas. She could only go on what had happened so far. They'd been wonderfully accommodating to her, and no one raised an eyebrow about her profession—not a single snide comment about a woman in a man's sport, or ignorant question like, "Do you wear lingerie when you play?"

As far as she could tell they were sincere and normal, despite the scars she couldn't see.

M. J. listened to them while she ate. She watched them, too—watched the way they interacted with the people they loved. Jordon and Grey seemed happy, authentic, and capable of maintaining long-term relationships. It gave her hope for Tag. Maybe he could work through all of this and have no use for the emotionally guarded man she'd first met. Maybe that man had gone away for good. She hoped so, because he was no match for the multi-dimensional man she'd discovered underneath—*that* man was the kind of man she could fall for.

M. J. was still thinking off and on about what that actually meant as they headed toward home again. Hadn't she already fallen for Tag to a certain degree? What came next? Love? She swallowed a scoff. Only twenty-four hours ago she'd decided it was worth another shot to have a man *and* a football career. Love was the longest shot of all.

What was so great about love anyway? If her parents were any example, love meant control. Being asked to compromise yourself, to be a shell of who you really were, just to conform to someone else's idea of how you should be. Just to make some man who wasn't comfortable in his own skin happy.

Well, thanks, but no thanks.

And yet, Tag had never even hinted that he wanted her to change.

Maybe he could be different.

"That went well," Tag said. Light from outside the car flickered across his face. He wasn't smiling, but he looked peaceful.

"It did. I like them."

He nodded, eyes on the road. "Me, too."

"Did you like them when you were younger?"

"I idolized them." The words sounded stuck in his throat.

What kind of father drove a wedge like that between sons? And in the name of baseball? Sick. M. J. wasn't about to pose those questions to a clearly overwhelmed Tag. "Now what?" she asked instead.

"We should be home around ten. Why? Is Tanya worried about you?"

It wasn't exactly the answer M. J. was looking for, but she ran with the lighter subject matter. "I think she likes the break. She's always yelling at me for making messes, leaving dishes in the sink, and throwing my clothes on the floor."

Tag grabbed her hand and dragged it into his lap, rubbing his thumb across her knuckles, blanketing her arm in a sprawling heat. "Then you should come home with me. I'll never complain about you throwing your clothes on the floor." He grinned as he brought her hand to his mouth.

Yeah, if he kept this up, she was bound to find out what came next, because she couldn't seem to stop falling.

• • •

A thick ribbon of sunlight spilt the kitchen in half, illuminating M. J. as she leaned against the sink, clutching a cereal bowl, talking about reading defenses, flex versus blitz to be exact. Tag wasn't the least bit interested in football strategies, but he listened in earnest and with a smile on his face, because he wanted her here, like this, in his T-shirt, standing in his kitchen, spooning up cereal as she talked about sports.

He'd woken up a different man, a lighter man, a man with an amazing woman and two brothers in his life. If he was dreaming this peace after the upheaval of the last month, he'd kill anyone who was stupid enough to pinch him.

"So practice tonight should be brutal." She rinsed her bowl and placed it on the top dishwasher rack, like she cleaned up after herself all the time, which he knew she didn't, because she told him so last night.

"Why are you doing that?"

She blinked at him. "Doing what?"

"Loading my dishwasher."

She shrugged. "Because it's polite."

"And you worry about being polite?" He stood and walked to her, wrapping arms around her waist.

The shake of her head was slow, considering. "Not usually."

"That's what I thought." He laughed against her neck, kissing her below the ear. "I have to go. Take your time. Just hit the garage button when you leave … and call me after practice."

An hour later, Tag was late for his first patient by the time he reached the office, held up by wandering lips and hands. It was hard to complain about a setback like that, which marked another change in him. Normally, getting a late start on his appointments was enough to ruin his mood for twenty-four hours. He couldn't imagine anything being powerful enough to dissipate the joy he was feeling now.

Shortly after lunch, Tag discovered the one thing that could.

"Dr. Howard, my name is Paul Burkett. I'm with ESPN radio, and I'm putting together a story about Grey Kemmons's recovery and return to baseball, of which I understand you've been an integral part. I'd love to talk to you about this miracle procedure. If you could give me a call …"

Tag swallowed a surge of uneasiness wrapped in excitement. This was the kind of acknowledgement he'd hoped for, but it was complicated. Was he supposed to freely admit the familial connection? Definite progress had been made where his brothers were concerned, but was he ready for a public admission?

Not when his parents didn't know about any of this. Tag needed to talk to them.

Staring at the phone, he took a big open-mouthed breath. His mother was out of the country, and his father was at the office. It would be impossible to get them together on the same call at this time of day.

He listened to Paul Burkett's voicemail again. The man was a sports reporter. Surely he was more interested in Grey's career than uncovering some tabloid story. Tag was twisting this. When he straightened it out, all he saw was a story about the grafting procedure being used successfully on a major league baseball player. And that story would fast track the professional accolades Tag had been looking for in the first place.

He could call the man first. There had to be some lead time to the story, and that would give Tag plenty of time to talk to his parents.

"Your two o'clock cancelled." Tammy poked her head into his office. "Maybe you can catch up on some of those dictations."

Tag smiled. His lack of efficiency with dictations was a consistent joke around here. "Actually, I have a call to make."

It was better to tackle these things head-on rather than let them fester.

As it turned out, Paul Burkett was a talkative, exuberant man. He ate up the details about the procedure, conjecturing about other injuries in the history of sport that could have benefited from regenerative grafting. Fifteen minutes in, and Tag's worries seemed for naught.

"Man, this is going to be great. Dynamite stuff. You're an impressive guy, Dr. Howard, and I have a feeling we're going to be hearing a lot more about you." Tag liked the sound of that. "Now, one last thing … was there more riding on the outcome of this procedure knowing that Grey Kemmons was your brother?"

Tag's ego shattered like a weak ankle, splintering fresh pain to his heart. This was exactly what he'd feared, an exposé. How could he think it was anything less after Paul waited until the very end of the interview to spring it?

He straightened his back and lifted his chin. "I'd love to talk more. I would." *Liar.* "But I already put myself behind schedule by talking to you this much. Maybe we could pick up later?"

"Sure. Sure thing. You name the time."

After I talk to my parents, that's for damn sure. But Tag kept that sentiment to himself and assured Paul he would call again soon.

Later that evening, Tag sat across the dinner table from Dad, trying to find the words to explain the situation. Telling Dad about Grey's injury and subsequent treatment was the easy part compared to telling Dad why it took Tag so long to say anything.

"Your mother says if they proceed with the sister-school plan, we'll all be expected to visit Africa as ambassadors. Of course, I immediately asked if there were golf courses in Africa, which didn't go over too well." Dad laughed.

Simon Howard was a polished man, about as opposite from Francis Kemmons as one could get. Short, wide, cerebral, and clumsy, the idea of Simon giving up on a child was ridiculous. Certainly, he wouldn't now. And somehow that made Tag's silence all these weeks worse.

"Dad, I have to tell you something."

Simon stopped chewing and propped his silverware on the edges of his plate. "That sounds serious."

"It is."

A slow smile crept across his wrinkled face. "You've met someone, haven't you? Your mother will be thrilled."

An instant image of M. J. popped into Tag's head. "Actually, yes, I have, but that's not exactly what I wanted to tell you. I mean, I'll tell you about that, but later."

"Okay. Now I'm extra curious. Is it about work?"

Tag nodded. "You could say that."

The rest of the story about Jordon and Grey flowed from there. Dad remained quiet throughout. The more Tag talked, the easier the words came, until he broached the subject of the interview.

The idea of airing his dirty laundry to the world wrapped tight around his gut. The idea of being seen as anything other than Simon and Edna's son thickened his sadness.

"Can I talk?" Dad asked, his courtesy the product of living with an outspoken woman for forty-two years.

"Of course." Tag was eager to stop talking, but he was less eager to hear what Dad had to say. What if Tag had disappointed him with the way he'd handled things?

He never wanted to disappoint his parents.

"First, I wish your mother was here, because you know she would have a lot to say, and those words would be invaluable." He smiled. The softness of his face was reassuring. "Second, I've wondered when something like this would happen. One of those boys was bound to want to find you—if it wasn't you wanting to find them. All normal. So, what now, right?" Tag nodded. "You have these brothers who remind you of things you'd rather not think about, and you have a reporter who wants to talk about things you'd rather not talk about."

"Exactly." Tag's skin tingled with relief. He should've told them as soon as Jordon called.

"My advice? Talk to the reporter. Get it out there once and for all. You did nothing wrong. Be honest, and you have nothing to fear. Of course, you're a grown man, and you make your own decisions, so just know whatever you decide to do, it doesn't change how proud I am of you, my son." Dad's eyes sparkled with tears.

Tag was about to get out of his chair and embrace him, when Dad cleared his throat and said, "Now, tell me about this girl, because that's going to be the thing your mother grills me about."

After all that, it was incredulous to think Tag was smiling. "It's sort of crazy, but Mom already knows her from the school."

"You don't say? Is she a teacher?"

Tag shook his head. "She's a quarterback."

Dad's eyes widened. "An athlete. That suits you, doesn't it?"

It did, and Tag couldn't wait to tell M. J. that, to tell her everything, but first, he had another call to make. After dinner, he would call Paul and finish the interview, be honest, like Dad said. It wouldn't be easy, but it couldn't possibly be as hard as Tag's early life had been.

• • •

"Grey plays professional baseball. Jordon played professional baseball. In fact, in my research, I learned that your father acted as agent during both of their drafts. On the contrary, I couldn't find anything about you playing a single inning—not even little league. How does it feel to be the odd man out?"

From the start, Paul's questions had been more aggressive than Tag anticipated. Even the darkness inside Tag's home office didn't hide him from the pressure.

"I don't see myself that way." *Anymore.* He spoke carefully, because it was a new and shaky assertion, tested more and more with every question.

"Really? I'm surprised by that. You said you were given up for adoption when you were nine years old, but Jordon and Grey remained with your father. Don't you resent the things they shared and the life they lived without you? Birthdays. First days of school. Weddings and christenings."

Tag switched the phone from one sweaty hand to the other. "Jordon and Grey were estranged for many years, too."

"But not as many as you."

The reminder rankled. As well as things had gone in Pittsburgh, his brothers' solidarity was very apparent. Tag would never be as close with them as they were with each other. And that hurt— enough to make him wish it all away. Progress be damned.

He dipped the phone away from his mouth to clear his throat. "It is what it is."

"Come on. You have to wonder why they didn't contact you years ago. They were adults long before you were. They could've picked up a phone years before they needed you to heal Grey's hand. Don't you wish they had given you that courtesy?"

It was a harsh question, but it was a valid one, too.

Tag's jaw clenched. "Trust me." His voice hardened. "I wouldn't change a thing about my life. I wouldn't change places with anyone. I lucked out. My brothers ..." the word dripped with acridity, "didn't. I mean look at me. Look where I am. I have the perfect mother and father. Look what I've accomplished. My education and professional accomplishments are second to none. You tell me who's sitting pretty. They're successful, sure, but remember ultimately who fixed whom."

Silence fell over the line and Tag flinched, as his own defensive and still clearly bitter words registered. Damn it. He regretted ever dialing the phone.

"Very good, Dr. Howard. I believe I have all I need."

I bet you do. Tag closed his eyes, took a breath, and ended the call. He told himself that the worst was over. He didn't have to talk about this anymore. He was done. He would heal. He would move on. With M. J. His brothers could be there, too, on the periphery, but they weren't in town, and he didn't have to constantly think about them.

It sounded like a good plan—perfect really. Nevertheless, Tag spent the rest of the day ignoring his brain's insistence that once the interview went live there would be fall out.

Chapter Twelve

M. J. tossed her duffle bag in the open hatch beneath the touring bus and reached into her back pocket for her ringing phone.

"Ooh! Is that your yummy man?" Jillian asked with a cheesy grin. "*Doctor* Yummy."

"Maybe," M. J. answered with a laugh. She'd refused to spend last night with him, citing proper preparation for the game. He was probably calling to complain that the sheets were cold.

She glanced at the phone with a smile on her face, but the happy expression turned to shock when she saw the Caller ID. *Dad.*

"Hey," she said, pressing the phone to her ear as she boarded the bus, feeling the jumble of confusion and excitement in her gut. He rarely called. He never called near game day—that would mean he might have to talk about the sport he wished his daughter didn't play.

Maybe from all the post-game texts that went unacknowledged he'd realized she was on pace to break the league passing record and wanted to wish her good luck. Pigs didn't fly, but pigskin could.

"Maya …" For a split second that was all she heard. No matter how many times she told him she preferred the shorter, stronger version of her name, he insisted on using her more feminine, given name. But she would forgive that if he ever found it in his heart to follow *Maya Jane* with *I'm proud of you.* "It's your mother's birthday," he said instead. "I've been remiss at planning something. This trial is taking up all of my time, but I managed to make a reservation for dinner tonight. Of course, I want you to be there."

Of course. To think M. J. thought it remotely possible Dad was calling to say he was proud of her was pathetic. At twenty-seven years old, she should've known better. He should've known better, too. It was the middle of the season, and he hadn't even considered she might have a game when he made the reservation? Or was it worse than that? Had he considered it and deemed it unimportant enough to not matter?

The burn of tears trapped behind M. J.'s wide, stoic eyes as she claimed a seat with a despondent plop. "I can't. I'm on my way to Indiana for a game." Maybe it was immature, but she stressed that last two words.

He grunted, a sound that stuck between disappointment and disgust. "Well, then, could you at least text her and wish her well today?"

"Already did." Because she wasn't completely heartless when it came to them. They, on the other hand, could take a page out of their almighty good-manners book. "Maybe one of you could text me and wish me well, too? Indiana is a tough team, and I'm close to breaking a record."

His exhale echoed. "You know we want what's best for you."

"Does that include football?"

"You have more to offer the world than bartending and barbarism."

"There's more to football than barbarism, Dad. I wish you could see that."

"I have to go."

Of course he did. God forbid they have an extended conversation about what mattered most to M. J.

She ended the call, intent on settling her emotions and getting her head back on the game.

Tanya dropped into the seat beside her. "Hello, stranger."

M. J. rolled her eyes. "Cut the stranger crap. I slept at home last night, and I see you every single day at practice and the bar." She ticked off the places on an equal number of fingers.

"Those don't count."

"Why not?"

"Because we can't talk when you're sleeping, or practicing, or working.

M. J. stared at her best friend, who had a good point. They hadn't spent much quality time together lately. "Do you want to talk about something?"

Tanya shrugged. "Do you? Pop heard something on the radio yesterday. I was just wondering if it was true or if I need to get his head looked at."

The interview? It couldn't be. Surely Tag would've told M. J. when it aired. "I'm going to need more to go on than that."

"Pop said Doc is Grey Kemmons's brother." Tanya's eyes widened. "I told him it couldn't be true, because you would've told me already if it were. I mean, Grey Kemmons! You know how I feel about that boy. Second only to Yadi." She laid a hand over her breast.

M. J. sighed and sunk lower in her seat, knowing it would kill Tanya to find out M. J. had met Grey. But she didn't have the right to share Tag's heartache with other people.

The more pressing thing was the interview had aired, and Tag hadn't told her. That meant one of two things: either he didn't know it aired, or he knew, but he didn't want anyone else to know. If it was the latter, then why? And so much for being open and honest.

"Tag and Grey are brothers," M. J. said. "But that's really all I'm comfortable saying until I've talked to Tag. Just know it's not an easy topic."

Tanya nodded. "Okay, as long as you promise to get me in the same room with Grey as soon as you can. I want him to sign my jersey." She smiled and slid on her headphones.

M. J. stared out the window as the bus pulled away from the stadium. Rain splotched the pavement. She wasn't happy with how this trip started. First Dad's call, then Tanya's revelation, and now worry about Tag, all when M. J. needed to be focused on tomorrow's game.

An hour later, she was still stewing, and decided the best way to move on was to text Tag and get it out of the way: *Pop heard the interview. Did you know it aired?*

No response.

It was Friday, and he had patients. Maybe he was busy.

As the bus pulled into the hotel parking lot, her phone vibrated.

Tag: Yes, I did, but I don't want to talk about it.

So they were back to that.

Tag: You need to focus on your game.

Okay, she responded, even though nothing felt settled.

Instead of going out for a late dinner, M. J. feigned stomach upset, which wasn't a far reach. Alone in her room, she gave in and called Tag. She wasn't going to be able to focus on anything else until she talked to him.

Her call went straight to voicemail.

Dammit!

She used her phone to search the internet and find a podcast of the interview. Instinct told her what she was about to hear wouldn't be good. She curled into herself, but pressed play.

At the one-minute mark, the interviewer asked, "Are you a Kemmons?"

"I'm a Howard," Tag said.

"But you're a Kemmons by birth."

"Yes."

"But you're not a Kemmons in name."

"I was placed in foster care when I was nine."

Even with apparent cuts for editing, the interview dragged on. On more than one occasion, M. J.'s finger itched to hit the stop button. With each belabored word, the foreboding grew. Tag knew the interview was out, didn't he? Was he trying to hide it from her? It was rough, but he seemed to be holding his own against the pointed questions.

Suddenly, Tag's hardened voice cut through M. J.'s mental meanderings. "You tell me who's sitting pretty. They're successful, sure, but remember ultimately who fixed whom."

M. J. squeezed her eyes shut and hit "stop." She couldn't listen anymore. Those were the words of a defensive, arrogant man, not the man she'd come to know. No wonder he didn't want to talk about it.

Tough.

She called him again, undeterred by his voicemail. "I heard it. Please, call me. I'm worried."

Stop worrying, he texted. *I'm fine. Get some sleep. Focus on football. We'll talk after the game.*

If he was fine, he would've called her back.

She didn't sleep a wink.

• • •

Even though it had stopped raining overnight, the skies never cleared. M. J. didn't mind playing in overcast weather as long as her wideouts could catch. But by halftime, the sky seemed especially ominous. *Probably a sign.* She couldn't seem to shake the doom and gloom she'd been feeling since she got on the bus.

"Rooney, you good?" Coach asked as they jogged from the locker room to the field.

"Yes, sir," she said, avoiding eye contact.

"Good, because we need some points on the board if we're going to win."

There was a novel idea. She'd been telling herself and her teammates that the entire first half. "You got it, Coach. Points, coming right up."

And they did, only not for the Clash. M. J. fumbled on the thirty-yard line, which led to an Indiana field goal. As she sat despondent on the end of the bench, fear sliced through her. Worse than playing poorly was not being able to drag herself out of the hole she'd fallen into. There was no spark, no will to win, no matter how hard she tried.

She'd been fighting her whole life to prove she was good enough, and for the first time she wondered if she really was.

For the rest of the game, M. J. went through the motions with little efficiency. If it weren't for a Clash interception returned for a touchdown, they would have lost. Because of her. It was that bad.

"Rooney, shake it off," Coach said. "A win's a win."

It was true, but it wasn't comforting. She didn't want to be a liability to her team, and the past two games, that's exactly what she'd been, because she was trying to have it all, a respectful relationship with her father, a romantic relationship with Tag, and a successful football career.

Something was going to have to give, and it wasn't going to be football.

• • •

The last time Tag covered a Sunday game, M. J. fell out of the stands and changed his life. Hell, so much more than his relationship status had changed, and those changes were overwhelming.

"Grey Kemmons is your brother?" Rinaldi walked into the training room dressed in nothing but his sliding shorts. "I played with him in Triple-A. Great guy."

Tag nodded.

"Jordon Kemmons played ball, too, right?" Rinaldi asked while he climbed onto a table for his pregame massage. "Did you play?"

"Nope."

The therapist glanced at Tag, and even that tiny bit of eye contact felt judgmental, which made Tag turn and walk away before anyone could ask why he hadn't played the sport that was tantamount to a religion in the Kemmons family. He'd been fielding questions about his lineage since he arrived at the stadium, and he didn't want to talk about it anymore. He'd said all he had to say. It was time to move on.

Too bad nobody else saw it that way.

All he'd wanted was some relief from the burden of carrying this information. Had he known he'd be answering the same questions over and over again for everyone he met, he wouldn't have opened his mouth to anyone in the first place. He couldn't even do his job without people bringing up the interview, and that made him wonder what people were really thinking. *Poor kid* was probably high on that list. Well, Tag wasn't poor and he wasn't a kid—not anymore. He had power. He controlled his life, and he could make his own decisions. Enough was enough.

Marc walked into the room, his gaze locked on Tag. "You never told me."

"I never told anyone," Tag said, wishing that would keep more questions at bay.

"That's a big secret to keep."

"It wasn't exactly a secret, more like an unnecessary topic."

"When I told you Kemmons texted for your contact information because he had a patient for you to see, you didn't think it might be necessary to say, 'Hey, Marc, thanks. By the way, he's my brother.'"

"No."

"Touchy subject."

"Did you listen to the interview?"

"No, Pratt told me."

It figured. Tag had gone from being an up-and-coming sports medicine guru to a topic of operating room gossip. "Apparently, he didn't tell you enough," he said. "And unfortunately for you, I'm done talking about it." Because it was Tag's life, and he could choose to end this conversation right here.

"Whatever, man." Marc shook his head and walked away.

Tag faltered for a second. His shoulders drooped. He was a better friend than that—he *wanted* to be a better friend than that—but this exposure festered like a raw wound in the center of his chest, and all he wanted to do was cover it, so it could heal.

Then cover it, he thought, rolling back his shoulders and plastering a smile on his face. He'd let the emotions settle, and then he'd find Mark to apologize.

After the baseball game, Tag pulled into his garage eager for a sanctuary that only a few days ago he expected would include M. J. Now he wasn't so sure. She'd heard the interview, and now it was time to talk about it. Where was the sanctuary in that?

After changing, he mixed a Goose and tonic, and then he sat, staring at the flickering television, wondering when the shit storm that had become his life would pass.

The knock at the front door surprised him. M. J. knew the garage code. On his way to the door, he flipped through a mental Rolodex of anyone else it could be. A reporter? His gut hardened, but with a blast of breath he told himself he was getting carried away. Still, he pressed an eye to the peephole. For some reason, his heart sank when he saw it was M. J.

"Did you forget the code?" he asked when he'd opened the door, careful to keep his smile.

"No, I, uh, just decided to come this way." She, however, wasn't smiling.

She was gorgeous in tight black pants and an oversized, colorful blouse belted at the waist. One sleeve slipped down her arm, revealing her smooth shoulder. If she didn't look so worried, strangling her keys and nervously biting her bottom lip, he'd have yanked her by the hand and pulled her in for a kiss.

"Is everything okay?" he asked, even though he knew it wasn't. Still, he forced a smile.

She studied him, the lip never getting a break from her gnawing. "You tell me."

"Everything's great … now," he said, giving in to the need to hold her, pulling her closer with an arm around her waist. He placed a kiss below her ear and waited for the peace to seep in.

She responded in kind, wrapping her arms around his neck, and for a minute, everything was perfect. Tag's mood soared on the realization they could move past the turmoil and concentrate on nothing but this.

"Why didn't you tell me about the interview airing?" she asked.

He lifted his face from her neck. "Because I didn't want to talk about it before your game. Honestly, I still don't want to talk about it. What's done is done."

"That worries me."

"It shouldn't. I'm fine."

"You didn't sound fine in the interview."

Tag released her and stepped away, just enough so he could breathe through the disappointment. He wanted one person who didn't see this pathetic mess when they looked at him. "It was hard to be hammered with those things. I said what I had to say to keep moving forward, and now I'm done."

She tilted her head and narrowed her eyes like she was looking for something written on his face. He had news for her. She wasn't going to find anything there, not anymore. He was done with the revelations, and he was happy to be wearing the mask again.

"Are you done with Jordon and Grey?"

He looked away from her.

"Tag, you've come so far in such a short time, don't turn around and go back to the way it was."

Going back was exactly what he didn't want. Why would he want to go back to a world where he wasn't good enough, where he was worse than a third wheel, where he was disposable?

"You don't understand," he ground out.

She sighed. "And I can't if you keep saying it's fine when it's clearly not. It's not fine if you can't talk about it like it's fine. Refusing to talk about it isn't progress. Talking about it honestly, owning it because it's a part of you, that's what you should be striving for."

He didn't want it to be a part of him, not when it was a constant reminder of how he wasn't good enough. All this reconnecting with Jordon and Grey seemed like the right thing to do when the rest of the world wasn't staring at Tag, wondering what was so wrong with him that his father gave him away in the first place.

Crossing arms over his chest, he countered, "So now you're my therapist?"

Her beautiful face hardened until the muscle in her cheek twitched. He welcomed her anger, because it was better than her pity.

"No," she said. "I thought I was someone you could be honest with. I'm starting to wonder if that applies to anyone in this whole wide world."

"I *am* honest with you."

"When it's comfortable and convenient. You never told me how harsh that interview got. We shared the same bed afterward, and you never said anything. Sex is supposed to be about intimacy and connecting with someone on the deepest level possible, but it wasn't, because you were holding out on me, and you would've continued to do so if Tanya hadn't told me about the interview being released. You were going to keep it from me. Weren't you?"

"No!" This was out of control. She was misinterpreting everything.

"Then tell me now. Tell me exactly how you felt then, and how you feel now."

He grimaced, the muscles in his face a reflection of the rest of his body. "Angry. I'm angry."

"At your father? At your brothers? At the interviewer?"

"At you," he hissed, because this wasn't the night he expected or needed. "Because you won't let it go."

She stepped to him, face to face, her breath hot against his mouth, and then she jabbed a finger into the flesh above his heart. "You're the one who won't let it go. And as long as you're holding onto it, I can't do this."

He gripped her wrist, the searing pain in his chest telling him the answer to his question before he even asked, "Do what?"

"Us," she whispered. "I almost blew that game. If it weren't for a touchdown scored by the defense, we would've lost, because of me, because my head and heart were here with you."

"I'm sorry," he said, reaching for her, getting as far as her waist before she backed away.

"I'm sorry, too. I thought it was worth a shot to see if we could make this work, but I can't be with someone who is in constant turmoil because he isn't proud of who he is."

Tag balked. He had plenty to be proud of, including a successful career and parents who loved him. So what if he was embarrassed by the rest? Why wasn't the man in front of her enough?

"I am proud of who I am," he said. "I'm proud of this man, and I don't need to integrate him with the sorry-ass kid he used to be."

She shook her head. "It's already integrated, Tag, and things like this will keep coming up over and over again until you deal with them head on. You can't pretend it isn't there."

Yeah, he could. He'd been pretending for twenty-five years, and if she didn't like it, then maybe it *was* better for her to go.

He could handle the pain of losing her. Twenty-five years ago, he'd lost even more.

Chapter Thirteen

A little before noon, M. J. padded on bare feet into Tanya's bedroom and sat on the end of the bed. The team had been out until the wee hours of the morning celebrating their by-the-teeth win, but M. J. had never caught up with them. She didn't feel like celebrating after what happened with Tag. So she came home, crawled into bed, and was sound asleep by the time Tanya rolled in.

Swinging her legs around, M. J. spread out on the foot of the mattress and stared up at the Fathead of Yadier Molina. His right cleat was peeling away from the ceiling. Ending it with Tag was the right thing to do. He needed time to process everything and learn to love himself, and M. J. needed space to focus on the rest of this season. They owed that to themselves. Maybe someday when he'd healed and she'd conquered the female professional football world, they could try again. At the moment, she wasn't feeling particularly optimistic.

"Did you pee the bed?"

Thank God for Tanya. M. J. smiled, but she didn't take her gaze off the St. Louis Cardinals catcher's intense mask-impeded face. "No. Just wanted some company."

The mattress bounced as Tanya sat up and scrutinized her. "What's going on?"

"I ended it with Tag."

"What happened?"

"He's got issues."

Tanya huffed a laugh. "Don't we all?"

It was true, and M. J. didn't begrudge him that. She'd been willing to help him work through those issues—to a certain degree. She just couldn't assume those issues and let them destroy her dreams. How could she lead a life that was all about authenticity when the man she was with was doing everything he could to hide a major part of himself?

"I can't do processed and perfect," she said.

"So stay away from American cheese?"

M. J. managed a chuckle.

"Hey," Tanya said, pushing back the covers and scooting lower on the bed. "I'd take processed and perfect if it came with regular sex, even though I'd rather have him." She pointed to the Fathead. "It's something to think about."

But M. J. wasn't like that. She couldn't ignore everything that was wrong in exchange for a little sex. It was a sucky time to realize she wanted more. "Sex isn't everything."

"Says the woman who's been getting it."

"I wanted it to be more," she said, still staring at the silly Fathead, wondering if male athletes worried about similar things, balancing careers and relationships, or if they just had sex like Tanya was proposing—no strings—because society raised them to believe they could and should.

"Like what?"

It was going to sound corny, but in the spirit of honesty, M. J. said it anyway. "I wanted something fun and easy, sure, but I also wanted someone to share every part of my life with."

"That's why you have me." Tanya nudged M. J.'s arm.

M. J. glanced at her, offering a small smile. "You know what I mean."

"I know."

Tanya curled up beside her, and M. J. felt a warm wash of gratitude soothe some of the pain. This unconditional love and support was so different from the tempered emotion she received from her parents.

She reached out and patted Tanya's arm.

Tanya slapped a hand over M. J.'s hand.

She'd get through this bumpy patch. She'd be better, stronger for the wear, too. Her time with Tag had highlighted a few important things. One, M. J. was so damned blessed to have Tanya in her life. Two, if M. J. lost her focus again, her teammates could carry her sorry ass for the win. Not that she was going to be making a habit of that. And three, she had to do something about her family hang-ups once and for all. She couldn't keep backing down or pretending the lack of support didn't matter.

M. J. showered, ate, and readied for a late-afternoon practice, while she contemplated her next step toward unflappable football focus. Dad's lack of interest in her athletic career hurt, and like it or not, it was threatening to distract her almost every game. All the pre-game glances at her phone, hoping he would call to wish her well. All the post-game texts, hoping impressive stats would sway him in her favor. They were covert and underhanded, because she'd never had the guts to tell him exactly how she felt. Oh, she fought for the right to play. She defended her decision and her team, but she never told him his lack of support and interest made her sad. Never.

The more M. J. thought about it, the more she wanted to do something about that. So, while Tanya watched *Sons of Anarchy* in the living room, M. J. snuck off to the back bedroom and called Dad. Of course, he didn't answer, but she refused to let that dissuade her from reaching out and being completely honest with him. It was time she practiced what she preached.

She'd told Tag things weren't fine if he couldn't talk about them like they were fine. Well, that applied to her and Dad, too.

After the beep, M. J. said, "It's me. Just wanted to say, 'Hi.'" Among other things. "Call when you get a chance."

She hung up and stared at the phone in her hand, wondering if Felicia wouldn't call back first. Wasn't that the way things normally worked?

A red light glowing over the email icon caught M. J.'s attention, and she clicked. It was a message from Coach—*Thought you'd like this*—and a forwarded link to a Cleveland sports blogger's post about her season and career.

Rooney is the kind of athlete who changes the game ... or in this case legitimizes it. When you watch her play it's not women's professional football; it's football—period. I challenge anyone to watch a game and walk away thinking anything else.

Satisfaction swept over her, warming her cheeks. She read the post over and over again until her eyes clouded with happy tears. Recognition like this was all she ever wanted. To be judged as an athlete playing a game, not as a woman playing a modified sport.

Like she'd done so many times before, she clicked the forward button and typed Dad's email address. But this time, her fingers flew over the keyboard, adding a personal note. When she'd finished, she'd written exactly what was in her heart: *I wish you would see me this way.*

It was a tall order for most men, but if this random sports fan with no connection to her could recognize her accomplishments, why couldn't her father? He didn't have to like football. Heck, she had a feeling Tag didn't like football, either, but he came to see her play, and he talked to her about the games. He did those things because football was important to her.

More tears, and this time, they weren't the happy kind.

For all Tag's faults, making her feel less about who she was or the game she played wasn't one of them. And that was so big—huge.

She doubted she'd ever find another man like that.

• • •

Tag wasn't hiding. He just wasn't in the mood to talk. The only person he wanted to talk to had walked away from him, because he didn't want to talk about what she wanted to talk about. It was such a convoluted mess.

He sat at the breakfast bar in his parent's house, staring at dictation charts, having burned a week's vacation rather than repeat Monday again. He'd thought he'd be safe at work. After all, the ladies who answered his phones, prepped his patients, and filed his billing didn't listen to sports radio podcasts. At least they hadn't, until Monday around noon, when Marc rolled in, flapping his lips about "Tag's brother" sealing another record-breaking deal, which led to the simple question, "Who's Tag's brother?" *That* led to the not-so-simple answer, "Jordon Kemmons."

Within an hour, everyone in his office had perused the transcript on line, and they were eager to let their opinions be heard.

"You're famous now," Leanne had said.

For the wrong thing, Tag had thought, but he'd made some quip about hoping his fifteen minutes whittled down to five, and then he'd called it an early day.

He never made it home, though. After a phone call to his mother, he'd ended up here with a desire to get away and stay away until everyone else had forgotten about him.

The mudroom door opened and closed with a soft thud.

"You have no idea how much I love coming home to you," Mom said, pressing a kiss on his cheek. She set her purse on the counter and smiled at him. "I feel like I should ask you, 'How was school? Do you have homework?'" She laughed.

Tag barely smiled at the nostalgic quip, but he'd take a research paper and studying for an AP biology exam over this stress any day.

"Did anyone call?" she asked, reaching for the refrigerator and disappearing behind the open door.

It was a loaded question. She wasn't really asking if the home phone rang while she was at work. She didn't want to know if Aunt Ginny or some political action committee called. She wanted to know if any more reporters called … or if Jordon or Grey called … or if Tag called them.

"All quiet," he said.

He had this ridiculous idea M. J. would call. And it was ridiculous, because it wasn't like he was calling her. He wanted to, but he kept hearing her words: *We would've lost, because of me, because my head and heart were here with you.*

Tag didn't want to be her liability.

"That's good." With her hands full of vegetables, Mom hit the front of the refrigerator door with her hip, closing the appliance. "Right?" She dropped the armful on the counter in front of him. "It means the hubbub is dying down. That's what you wanted. That's why you're here."

Tag nodded. When *Sports Illustrated* called two days ago wanting exclusive rights to the reunion story in print and offering a cover, Tag feared the worst was yet to come. But maybe that had been the peak. Maybe things would settle for good now.

Mom slid a cutting board and paring knife toward him. "Then why are your shoulders all bunched up? Why aren't you smiling with relief after two quiet days?"

Tag cut into a red pepper, decapitating the stem. "I don't know."

She eyed him like she used to when he was a kid, calm and steady, like she could wait all day for him to crack. "I think you do."

Of course he knew. Deep down, he was feeling guilty about more than letting M. J. walk away. He'd been avoiding Jordon and Grey, lumping their calls and voicemails with the unwelcomed contact of journalists, because he didn't want to face what they might have to say about the interview. Tag hadn't exactly been enthusiastic about claiming them as brothers … when they'd been nothing but enthusiastic to claim him … but only after twenty-five years. He'd let that fact hurt him too much during the interview, and he'd said things that downplayed the importance of the relationship they'd started to build. Worse, he'd made statements that could call into question his respect for them and their career choices.

He wished he could take back the bulk of what he said. He wished for a lot of things, lately, not the least of which was that he could be a strong, polished, impervious man who knew just what to say and when to say it. Instead, he was the kind of man who crumbled under pressure—just like his biological father always said he would.

You can't cut it, boy. Now, go away.

And that's exactly what Tag did. He cancelled patients, traded game coverage, avoided Jordon and Grey's calls, and let M. J. leave without pulling out all the stops to make her stay.

All these years, he was still listening to Francis Kemmons.

Tag dropped his head into his hands and shook away the disgust.

"What is it?" Mom asked.

He wanted so badly to say, "Nothing. I'm fine. Everything is okay," but he'd been trying to say those things for years, and they just weren't working. "I can't seem to forget him," he whispered. "Twenty-five years, and he's stuck in my head."

"Look at me." Mom stood beside him, lifting his chin with her hand.

"I'm sorry," Tag said, struggling to make eye contact. "For bringing this up again."

She wrapped him in a fierce hug. "You have nothing to be sorry about. *That* man, on the other hand, deserves an afterlife of tortuous reparation."

"I keep trying to remember one good thing he may have said about me to counter the bad and gain some ground again, but there's nothing. He knew me first. He saw the real me before you, before the surgery, before the private schools and money made me a Howard. If you take away all those things, am I who he said I am?"

Her fingers dug into his jaw as she held his gaze. "You listen to me. You are *my* son, it doesn't matter what *that* man thought about you or said about you. He was wrong. People are wrong all the time, every day, for reasons too numerous and complicated to list. All that matters is that you feel the truth right in here." With her free hand, she pointed to his heart. "We love you, all of you, even the parts you can't seem to love yourself."

Tag nodded slowly, his neck stiff from the heavy emotion stuck in his throat.

"And I want you to remember something else," she continued. "*That* man said there was no place for a boy like you in baseball. Well, *my* beautiful, precious son …" she released his jaw and smoothed her hand against his cheek, "he was wrong. You are living, breathing proof that he was wrong. Every time you walk into that clubhouse to cover a game, every time you work your magic and get another man, like your brother, back out on the field, I want you to remember he … was … wrong." Her voice was loud and shaking. "It's time you start living that way."

They were both crying, and it wasn't pretty. Tag wasn't proud of the moments that brought him here, but for the first time in his life, he felt her words as truth in his bones.

Francis Kemmons wasn't to blame for this mess. Tag was. He'd given a dead man way too much control.

"Thank you," Tag said, hugging her, feeling the familiar warmth and comfort surround him.

"No, thank you, for opening up and talking to me. I always said I wouldn't push you, because you'd talk more when you were ready. I also said that would be a day we'd rejoice, because then we'd have indisputable truth that you were rising so far above it, it would never hurt you again."

That was what M. J. had been trying to say.

Mom patted him on the shoulder as she returned to the vegetables.

Tag stared at the mangled pepper in front of him, and then he straightened his back and exhaled what remained of the emotion he'd been holding in. "Just so you know, I screwed things up with M. J., too."

Mom never looked up from the vegetables. "Then fix them." She made it sound so easy.

"I will. I want to, but I also want to make sure there are actions behind my words. You know, proof that I'm making progress with this, so she doesn't have to worry about being burdened or distracted again."

Mom smiled. "That sounds wise."

He was on a roll now; filled with a strength he didn't know he had. "And I need to restore any goodwill lost between me and Jordon and Grey."

"Good man."

There again, Tag needed a plan—more than an apology.

His phone buzzed against the counter. Before he even looked at the number or name, he determined to answer it. He was done hiding.

"Unknown Caller," he announced, exchanging reassuring glances with Mom before he answered with a steady, "Hello."

"Dr. Howard?"

"Yes, it is."

"Neil Forest from *Sports Illustrated*. Do you have a minute?"

Tag's stomach flipped, but he stayed the course, because he did, in fact, have a minute—more actually. Tag would devote every waking minute to making things right.

Chapter Fourteen

"Two more games," M. J. yelled above the noise in the locker room as she slapped her hand against the inspirational words above the door and jogged into the hallway.

Her teammates roared behind her.

If they won the next two games, they'd have home field advantage. Good things happened on home turf. She repeated that like a mantra all through warm-ups, feeling loose and ready, which was a plus when she took the first hit. Being loose meant M. J. absorbed the blow and bounced back without too much fanfare. She preferred the crowd noise to come from plays like the thirty-two-yard touchdown pass she dealt to Janie down the leftfield line.

Unfortunately, that was the last time the Clash made it anywhere near the red zone in the first half. M. J. wished she could say the same for Buffalo, who'd sacked her twice and hurried her every play in between. She glanced at the scoreboard on her return from the locker room. *21-7.*

"We are not out of this." She went down the line, slapping every helmet on the way. "These people came to see a win. Let's give it to them."

She pointed up at the stands, her line of vision following. Somehow, in the spattering of people, she narrowed in on a familiar face. Dad.

"Shit," she whispered, vibrating with more than adrenaline now. He was here. He'd never even called or emailed back after she forwarded the link to the blog post.

Deep, shaky breaths moved in and out her mouth. She could not afford to get distracted by this. Not now. She needed to win.

Tamping down the emotion building in her chest, M. J. took a spot beside her offensive coordinator and locked her mind on football.

Eventually, the Clash's running game showed up, exploiting some cracks in the defense. They picked up some good yardage and added fuel to M. J.'s inner fire. Following two first-down conversions, she dropped back to pass, releasing the ball in an arch up the middle to Jillian, who only had one woman to beat. She did so with flair. Juke, spin, and sprint.

"Touchdown Clash," the announcer bellowed, and then he recognized M. J. as the league-leading, record-breaking passer she'd just become.

Her feet seemed to hover above the turf, making the walk to the sideline slow and dreamy. She'd known she was close—maybe even somewhere in the back of her mind she knew the exact yardage she needed to make her mark—but until the announcer said it, the momentous moment hadn't sunken in. Now that it had, satisfaction tingled every inch of her overheated body, but then she saw the scoreboard. *21-14.* She didn't have time to bask if she wanted to win. *One possession to tie, two to take the lead.*

When M. J. reached the sideline, she stole a glance into the stands and waved at the cheering fans. When she did, she saw Dad, again. He wasn't smiling, but he was clapping. The small gesture meant something—even if it was nothing more than reflex. Hell, he could scowl and never move for the rest of the game … because he was here. He'd seen her record-breaking game.

As M. J. angled her body back toward the field, something pulled her focus to the far left grandstand and a smiling man who looked an awful lot like Tag. Okay, now she was seeing things. *It's football, Rooney, not a fairytale.*

The on-field whistle pierced her thoughts, drawing her back to the game.

By the two-minute warning, the score was tied. Two possessions later, they made a field goal for the win. Not until M. J. reached the locker room did she contemplate the magnitude of the game.

The Clash was one game away from clinching home field advantage in the playoffs. She was the current record holder for passing in the league. And Dad had seen it all. Emotion barreled through her, knocking her ass into the folding chair beside her locker, where she faced the wall of metal and released the energy in a burst of tears.

Teammates came and went, congratulating her, and M. J. hugged them all in return. She stayed at her locker long enough for her spirits to settle, and then she showered and dressed.

"Rooney, somebody's out here, waiting patiently for you."

It was then that M. J. remembered the man who looked like Tag. Anticipation picked at her damp skin. If she wasn't conjuring him, if he was really there, it would be just like him to stay and greet her—he'd done it before. Despite what happened between them, despite all the reasons she knew it was for the best, she couldn't think of anyone she wanted to see more after this game.

Securing her damp hair with a clip atop her head, she belted her tunic, zipped her boots, and came face to face with Dad instead.

"Good game," he said.

M. J. felt faint, so overwrought with emotion her limbs went numb. Discovering Dad in the stands was one thing. Finding him waiting for her to tell her *good game* had to be a dream.

"Thank you," she said, stuck by the sudden urge to look around for Tag, expecting her fairytale evening to keep producing. But he wasn't there. Maybe he never had been.

A fleck of disappointment marred the moment. She was being greedy, wasn't she? This should be enough.

"How about dinner?"

Dad's invitations were far and few between, so M. J. nodded. "I'd like that."

She followed him to the country club and parked beside him in the lot, gripping the steering wheel, breathing deeply, trying to settle her stuttering pulse. The entire drive she'd been pondering what came next. She couldn't remember sharing a meal alone with her father since childhood.

By the time M. J. was seated at the table, she decided everything she wanted to achieve when this season began was within reach, including respect and legitimacy in the eyes of her father.

"Thanks for coming to the game," she said. "It means a lot to me."

Dad nodded and studied his menu like it was evidence set before him in trial.

His distance was a letdown, but she reminded herself he came to the game, acknowledged she'd played well, and asked her to dinner. They were steps in the right direction.

"The flounder is good," he said.

Having hated fish her whole life, M. J. suppressed a juvenile gag. Why would he even say that now? He had to know she wasn't going to take the hint. When M. J. had been growing up, there'd been actual arguments, culminating in groundings, over her refusal to eat Felicia's fish dinners.

She was never going to understand him.

Though M. J.'s shoulders slumped, she refused to pick apart the interaction anymore. He came to the game. He asked her to dinner. *Steps in the right direction*, she thought again.

They ordered—him, flounder, her, the biggest burger she could find—and then she waited, patiently, to talk about the game in detail. Surely they'd broach the subject. She was the league-leading passer. How could they not talk about it? But he'd gotten a new car, and a new case assignment, and when they were done "discussing" those things, his phone distracted him.

"Pardon me," he said, dipping into his interior jacket pocket and looking at his phone. Whatever he saw prompted a smile, a smile M. J. hadn't seen directed at her in … years.

Was she really that displeasing?

"That's wonderful news," he said as he stared at the screen, his smile widening. "You owe your mother a congratulatory call or text. She's just been named chair of the ballet's yearly gala."

M. J. halted a sigh with a gulp of ice water. The evening nosedived. She would never understand why one woman's accomplishments were touted over another's. Why was M. J. expected to jump with praise for Felicia's chairwomanship, but no one was expected to do the same for M. J.'s accomplishments?

"Did you tell her to text me?" M. J. asked impulsively.

Dad blinked as he returned his phone to his pocket. "I'm not sure I'm following you."

"I broke a long-standing, league record tonight. Did you tell Felicia about that? Did you tell her to congratulate me?"

"Maya Jane, I don't know where you are going with this, but wherever it is, it's not looking good."

"I'm just tired of the double standards."

He snorted, a move that lowered his eyeglasses to the tip of his nose. Some men did not look good in glasses. They looked arrogant and judgmental. Again, she thought of Tag, wishing he'd been waiting for her after the game, instead.

"Nonsense," Dad said. "You're the one who chose to live a life that was bound to come with resistance."

"Who's resisting? Not me, not the cheering fans in that stadium today." To think Dad had been among them, and still, he didn't get it. "The only people resisting are my parents. How sad is that?"

His bushy, gray brows lowered enough to darken his eyes. "I was there, Maya Jane. I said good game. What more do you want from me?" He didn't pause for an answer. "This has never been about your talent as an athlete. This is about ... your refusal to grow up and take your place in productive society." He looked sick, pale, and beads of sweat speckled his forehead. He dabbed at them with his napkin. "Your mother … never would've played past what was acceptable."

It had always been so damn hard for him to talk about M. J.'s mom.

"What was acceptable for a woman," M. J. corrected, cringing. "You wouldn't be saying this to me if I were a man."

He pushed back his tonic water and smiled at the waiter approaching with his fish.

While M. J. picked at her fries and poked at her burger, she tried to look like everything was fine, like she wasn't bothered by the abrupt end to their football conversation, like she was interested in the safe-to-share details from Dad's latest case, but all the while her brain raged about what had happened here. No progress. No fairytale ending in which Dad declared he was her biggest fan. This was always going to be an issue between them for whatever reason, wasn't it?

He'd been at the game. He'd acknowledged her stellar play. He'd invited her to dinner. So what? She could see the acts for what they were now: obligation, not enthusiasm. And that was fine with her. She'd been playing and performing all these years without his glowing approval. Nothing had to change. She'd just go back to pretending it didn't matter.

It's not fine if you can't talk about it like you're fine. Those were her over-simplistic words when she'd walked out on Tag. She'd stopped seeing him, because he'd rather pretend everything was okay than fight to make it okay. Ha! Well, what the hell was she doing right now?

She was a hypocrite, and she owed Tag an apology. But first, she needed to finish what she started here.

"Dad," he looked up from his fish, "Your disapproval really hurts me. You have to make a better attempt to accept me for who I am, or I'm going to stop attempting to have a relationship with you. I'm not going to change. What you see is what you get. Love it … or lose it." She pushed away from the table, but not before she snagged the last bit of burger off her plate. "Thanks for the meal."

•••

Sunday morning, Tag woke in his own bed in his own house. It was good to be looking life in the eyes again. Of course, it would be better to be looking in M. J.'s eyes again.

She'd given a brilliant performance yesterday, and he'd wanted to tell her so. He'd tried after the game, waiting in the shadows outside the locker room, not knowing if she'd want to see him or what he'd say when she did. Congratulations seemed like a reasonable place to start, but he never got a chance. Tanya came out of the locker room, loudly greeting an older man, who'd been standing by the door. Hearing the man addressed as Judge Rooney was all it took for Tag to know it was M. J.'s father. Since Tag couldn't figure out how he'd fit into that mix, he'd walked away.

Now, he wished he'd waited for her.

Launching out of bed, Tag ran several miles and then returned to the condo to shower and prepare for an afternoon baseball game. Maybe he could call M. J. to congratulate her. Of course, he wanted to see her again, and hoped the contact would reveal she wanted to see him, too. But after that game, and at this point in her season, he didn't want to add more pressure.

Twice, he picked up his phone and stared at her contact information. How much pressure would one call add? While he contemplated the answer, Jordon called. They'd been playing phone tag for days.

"Hey." He'd already talked to Grey and apologized, but he worried gruff Jordon would take things harder.

"My apologies for the runaround I gave you. I was out of the country."

"No apology necessary—at least not from you. Have you talked to Grey?"

"I listened to the interview."

Of course he did. Nothing baseball-related got past the sport's sharpest agent.

"I'm sorry," Tag said, rubbing the base of his throat. "I got angry at some things the interviewer said, and I made defensive comments about you and Grey that I regret. I screwed up."

Jordon grunted. "Listen, if you were my client, I'd have prepped you good and hard before you talked to that man, and you would've expected his questions and attitude. You didn't have me then, so you faltered, but you have me now—as a brother, if that's what you want. I don't blame you for the words you said in an interview. I'm not an idiot, man. I knew this wouldn't be easy. Why do you think I waited so long to call? How can I fault you for your missteps when I was a fucking coward?"

Tag sat on the bed with his muscles gone slack. Crisp, clear air tingled in his lungs. "Thank you for understanding. I appreciate it, and I want to do something to fix things. *Sports Illustrated* called me and Grey, so I'm assuming they called you, too. I want us to do the cover story."

"I appreciate the show of solidarity, but I'm not sure I'm a cover model."

"I disagree!" A woman sing-songed in the background.

Maggie. Tag smiled. A pang of longing struck beneath his breastbone as he imagined Jordon and Maggie's Sunday morning spent laughing and snuggling with Braydon. Grey and Nel were probably walking the dogs. Which led him right back around to M. J.

Jordon chuckled as he tried to talk Maggie into leaving the room. Her powers of persuasion were better than Tag's, because soon Jordon said, "Fine. I might not see myself as a cover model, but I am a businessman who makes an awful lot of money based on image. This cover story could be valuable publicity for my business."

Tag smiled. "So you'll do it?"

"I suppose I could suffer for my bottom line.."

"He has a very nice bottom line," Maggie yelled.

Jordon shushed her, and Tag laughed. "I really don't want to think about how nice your bottom line is or isn't."

"Ditto. Listen, if we're going to do this thing, I'm going to push to have the shoot here at the lake. I've been gone a lot lately, and I don't want to add another trip to the schedule. M. J. is welcome here, too."

The pang grew, paralyzing Tag's lungs. "Thanks, but she … only has one game left before playoffs. There's no way she'd take time off at this point."

"Hey, there's nobody better to understand and admire that than me. I just wanted the offer on the table."

"Thanks, man." Tag was chickening out again, wasn't he? He should come clean, tell Jordon the truth. "You know, in the spirit of honesty, M. J. and I aren't seeing each other anymore."

There. Tag said it, but he didn't feel fine about it.

"That sucks."

"Yep."

"Anything I can do?"

Tag actually smiled. He wasn't sure why. Maybe it was just nice to share the shit parts of life and have someone to commiserate with. "I'll let you know if I think of anything."

When the call ended, Tag finished dressing. An odd sense of satisfaction surrounded him even though his life was far from perfect. That had to be a first. Again, he thought of calling M. J. He'd congratulate her, and then he'd tell her about the progress he'd made. Hell, he'd thank her, because she opened his eyes in the first place. Yeah, he was definitely going to call her.

But M. J. beat him to it.

Tag smiled at his ringing phone, feeling the vibration shoot up his arm and straight to his heart. She'd been thinking about him, too.

"Hello," he said, not bothering to suppress his enthusiasm.

"Hi."

Her soft breathing lingered, making it the sweetest silence he'd ever heard.

"Congratulations on the win and breaking the record. You were beyond amazing in that game."

"You were there!" She sounded so damned pleased. Now, he really wished he'd stayed.

Tag would've weathered meeting her father if he could've seen her excitement in person. "Of course, I was there. I wouldn't have missed it."

She was quiet again. "I thought it was you, but I couldn't be sure, and then you didn't stay."

"I stayed for a little bit, but then I saw your dad, and, well, he was there first."

She sighed. "I wish it had been you."

Her words were laced with pain, and a moment that should've been filling him with even more joy twisted. "I'm sorry."

"Could we meet someplace … to talk?"

He wanted nothing more than to drop everything and run to her, but he'd dropped everything for an entire week, and he had some making-up-for-it to do. "I have to cover a baseball game, but I'm free this evening."

"I have to work, and then I'm sparring with Tanya."

"I can come to you. At work."

"Like old times." He could hear her smiling through the words. *Old times.* "That wasn't that long ago."

"Too long," she said.

It was. He missed the way she plied him full of watered-down vodka tonics and pushed him outside his comfort zone. Good things happened out there.

"I'll see you tonight," he said.

Tonight couldn't get here fast enough.

Chapter Fifteen

Of course, the game went into extra innings, which frustrated Tag, but the minute he sat on a wooden stool at Mama Mary's bar, he settled. And the minute M. J. handed him a vodka tonic with a sparkling smile, he shed all the aggravation he'd accumulated trying to get here.

"Evening, stranger," she said.

There was just enough time for that husky voice to wash him in warmth before she turned her back and tended to another customer. For a Sunday, this place was busy—too busy for a meaningful talk.

What exactly did she want to talk about anyway?

Tag had his hopes up for one thing: she wanted to be with him again. He was realistic enough to know that might not happen. All that mattered was that she called, and he was here, which meant he'd been given a chance to make things right.

Sipping his drink, Tag watched her pour a draught. Dressed in a black T-shirt and dark jeans that clung to her lean body, she tempted him like nothing and nobody ever had. His gaze locked on the boots, and he hoped beyond reason she'd worn them on purpose, knowing she was going to see him.

She passed out drinks, filled a waitress's order, and then returned. "Sorry. It's busier than I thought it would be." She pushed a strand of hair off her face, tucking it behind her ear.

The simple action flexed her triceps, the same muscles Tag had seen contract every time she delivered a perfect spiral. "It's all good," he said. "I'm enjoying my drink." He lifted his glass for emphasis. "And the view."

Maybe that last part was uncalled for. After all, they hadn't agreed to anything more than meeting and talking. He was getting ahead of himself, but it had always been that way with them. He opened his mouth to apologize.

M. J. glanced down at her boots and smiled, stopping his words.

A passing waitress called out for a beer. "Hold that thought," M. J. said to him, and she winked.

Desire rocketed through him, warming his skin until he had to tuck a finger beneath the collar of his shirt for some air. What was happening here? It was like someone pressed rewind, running the tape straight past all the ugly parts that had ripped them apart. M. J. didn't seem like a woman who "couldn't do this," and he sure wasn't a man who wanted to keep his distance from her. Could it be this easy? Or were they setting themselves up for disappointment again?

A few minutes later, M. J. was back with a fresh drink for him and some time to spare. The bar had cleared. The rest of the room turned quiet.

She propped elbows on the wooden ledge and watched him drink. "I'm sorry."

"Don't be. It's your job, and I'm a big boy. I know how to wait patiently."

She moved closer, until her fingertips traced the bony bump of his wrist, flaring the need already building inside him.

"That's not what I meant," she said. "I'm sorry for being a hypocrite that night at your place. I called you out for wanting to pretend everything was okay, and then I realized I was doing the same thing with my dad. It was a rude awakening, and you deserve to know that."

He watched her pull her bottom lip between her teeth as her gaze wandered.

"What happened with your dad?"

She exhaled long and loud. He would've felt guilty about pushing her to talk if she hadn't moved on to playing with his hand, tracing his fingers, up one side and down the other, lingering in the webbing before traveling up again.

Tag's breath was slow and low to prevent a shudder.

"He came to the game," she said. "And then, he took me to dinner. But in the end he made it abundantly clear he didn't enthusiastically support my career choices, so I gave him an ultimatum, and then I walked out."

Tag didn't get that guy. How in the world could the man who was half the creative team of someone as awesome as M. J. not brag about her from the rooftops?

"I'm sorry," he whispered.

She shrugged. "Me, too, but I'm done wasting energy on it. I have better things to do." She smiled as she squeezed his hand, but she was summoned by a customer a moment later.

Tag sat there reeling, wondering what her words meant for him, for them. Nothing she said changed the fact she was still in the middle of a critical football season. Would she want to pick up where they left off in spite of that?

By the time she came around again, Tag had decided it was worth a shot to be honest with her and find out exactly what happened next.

"I should've never let you leave that night, not like that," he said. "I should've told you everything about the interview, even before I talked to the interviewer. Maybe then I wouldn't have made such an ass out of myself."

She looked speculative for a moment, and he expected meaningful, sentimental words to come out of her mouth. "You have a really nice ass," she said, instead, and then spun around to fill another drink.

Tag was smiling, an expression that lifted more than the corners of his mouth. In the midst of a gritty bar on the "wrong side of town," there were no gaping holes inside of him begging to be filled. Just a quiet sort of peace he didn't want to live without. When he was with M. J., he was complete.

Again, he watched her work, pouring draughts, making change, and wiping the counter. Mundane tasks. But it didn't matter what she was doing, he could watch her do it all day, every day.

Maybe he loved her.

Tag swayed with the thought until his elbows hit the bar. He'd never been in love before. Love was raw, messy, dependent, and the absolute last thing a guy who hated being honest with himself wanted.

But he wasn't that guy anymore, was he?

"How are Jordon and Grey?" M. J. asked, when she came around again.

"Good. I apologized for the interview, and I decided to back up my words with action."

She grinned. "I like action."

"Who do you think I learned that from?" This time, Tag reached for her, grabbing onto both of her hands. "I'm going to do another interview, but this time *with* Jordon and Grey. For *Sports Illustrated.*" Her eyes widened as she squeezed his hands. "They're going to put us on the cover."

"Shut. Up." She swatted his hands away, laughing the whole time. "That is so cool."

Tag nodded, again feeling stuffed with joy. He wished he could bottle it, and save it for the days and weeks following the magazine's release, when everybody would want to talk about his past all over again.

He wanted to believe he'd handle things differently this time, but how could he be sure?

The rest of the evening unfolded in much the same way— stolen moments of conversation interrupted by drink requests. Somehow, Tag got away with only two drinks of his own, probably because he spent more time watching M. J. than he did drinking and staring at the overhead TV.

When her shift was over, she left him briefly to sign out and grab her sweatshirt. He still didn't know exactly where he stood with her, but he knew where he wanted to stand. She'd become an enormous part of his happiness, and he hoped to do the same for her—even if that meant keeping things friendly but contained so she could get through the rest of the football season without distraction.

He never wanted to hurt her again.

M. J. met him at the front door, and Tag fully expected her to bid him goodnight. She'd mentioned sparring with Tanya at the gym. Instead, after eyeing him up in a way that had his temperature rising, she said, "If you don't have anywhere else to be, you're welcome to come to the gym with me."

If he'd had somewhere else to be, he would've cancelled. Holding the door open for her, he smiled. "I'd like that. Maybe I'll get to see Pop and Dante." He'd also get to walk a block with her in those boots.

That was the biggest bonus of all.

Outside on the street with the evening sun highlighting everything in a dull red, Tag settled into easy steps beside her. In sync. Again, he thought about love.

"You know, I've been thinking maybe we could try again." She said, glancing at him, then quickly looking away.

"What about football?"

"What about it?" Her lips quirked. "It's a part of me, and you're the only man I've ever met who accepts that without question. I like coming out of that locker room and seeing you. So I think we should give it another try ... if you want to."

This time when she looked at him, he was ready with a smile that held her gaze. "I want to."

She nodded. "Good. Because I figured since we're both working through family issues why not work on them together? Teamwork, you know?" She grinned. "I like being part of a team as long as I can pretty much run it." She lowered her shoulder and bumped him.

He caught her and didn't let go, winding his arm around her waist and holding her there, feeling her hip move in alignment with his, hearing the soles of her boots meet the pavement when his shoes did. Perfect synchronicity. Again, he thought about loving her, and this time, he knew without a shadow of a doubt he did.

She liked being part of a team, which boded well for them as couple—if he didn't screw things up again by holding things in. With one exception. It didn't feel wise to tell her he loved her, yet. He needed to sit with it, and then sit *on* it. At least till the season was over. She didn't need to know just how serious he was about her, about them, not with playoffs on the horizon. Agreeing to give this another shot was enough … for now.

Tag hugged her tighter, until she dropped her head to his shoulder and he rubbed his nose against her silky hair. He loved her, and keeping that information to himself wasn't going to be easy. He only hoped if he cracked—when he cracked—he didn't ruin everything.

•••

With two home games in a row, it already felt like the Clash had home-field advantage. That didn't mean M. J. wasn't nervous, especially when Tanya informed her that the swelling crowd included not only Tag, but her parents.

Her gut churned. Her pulse raced. And every one of her senses twitched on high alert. She hadn't spoken to her father since she walked out of their indigestion-plagued dinner, but by his appearance at the game—with Felicia, no less—M. J. couldn't help but assume he was willing to make the attempt she'd asked of him.

The jackrabbit tendency stuck with M. J. throughout the first quarter, making her passes hasty and woefully inaccurate. Fortunately, Toledo's offense hadn't found their rhythm yet, either.

"Settle down," Tanya said in the huddle, tapping the forehead of her helmet against M. J.'s. "You got this."

"I got this," M. J. repeated.

In the end, she barely did, but a win was a win, like Coach had said. And lo and behold, it was sinking in. This was her lowest-yardage game of the season without a passing touchdown to her credit. The fact that she'd run into the end zone for the win soothed the sting a little bit.

Once she was showered and changed, she waded through back slaps and "good games" to reach the locker room exit, knowing this time Tag would be waiting, wondering if her parents would be waiting, too. Suddenly, there wasn't any thought in the world that could sooth M. J.'s anxiety.

When she pushed outside, the three of them stood together like old friends.

"Great game," Tag said, taking her hand and kissing her on the cheek, the warmth of the action momentarily blocking her fear. "I met your parents."

And it was back, picking up the hair on her neck. Still, M. J. smiled. "Cool. My own personal cheering section." Hadn't she always wanted that?

This one included a woman in blush linen pants and a silky tank top, her hair in a sleek bun, along with two men clad in golf course attire. M. J. didn't want to see a single similarity between her father and Tag, but it was there, and she wondered what would happen if she looked closer. Would she find more?

M. J. looked away. "Good game," she called to Jillian.

"Why didn't you tell us you were dating a doctor?" Felicia asked.

It was ridiculous and annoying to think Tag's profession had come up in a matter of minutes. The question added to the already-tense thoughts in M. J.'s overtaxed brain. Dad and Tag had more in common than taste in golf shirts. They had high-powered, professional careers and education up the wazoo—things her father wished she had.

M. J. shrugged. "His profession's not important." At least not to her.

"Good game," Dad said with considerably less enthusiasm than Tag had said it with, but he said it—twice in one season—and it helped settle M. J.'s stomach.

"Thanks." The locker room door opened, and she stepped out of the way.

Felicia wrinkled her nose. "What's that smell?"

"Sweat," M. J. said, having heard the complaint before.

"The smell of victory," Tag said, squeezing her hand.

And just like that the similarities she'd been worrying about a few minutes ago paled in comparison to the one glaring difference. Tag supported her—always.

"Could we tempt you two with a dinner invitation?" Dad asked.

He really seemed to be trying to meet her demand. How could she turn him down without giving him a fair chance?

"What do you say?" she asked Tag with a bit of hesitation in her voice. She'd be perfectly happy if he had other plans. Her family had a way of bringing out the worst in her, and she didn't want Tag playing witness to that.

"I'd love to," he said with a smile.

Dad nodded. "Then, it's settled."

Or it would be. There was a lot riding on this meal.

. . .

Tag sat at an extended dining table in the lavishly decorated Rooney house. The paisley wallpaper hurt his eyes almost as much as the blinding light from the garish chandelier. He glanced at M. J. every chance he got for a reprieve.

She was busy frowning at her plate, picking at the salmon Felicia had served. Heck, after the way she'd fought to grind out a win, he'd have expected her to inhale whatever was on her plate. Then Tag remembered that M. J. hated fish. He was surprised her parents weren't aware of that.

"Dr. Howard, you'll have to come to the ballet gala this year. Did Maya Jane tell you I'm chairwoman?" Mrs. Rooney stared expectantly at Tag.

Tag cringed at her formal address. He was proud of his title and success, but in these surroundings, it felt pretentious. "Tag," he said. "Please, call me Tag. And congratulations."

"Thank you. Even though I gave up dancing years ago, ballet is still a passion of mine. I tried to pass along the love to Maya Jane, but she … well, she didn't give it a fair chance."

"I agreed to one year of lessons, because I read that Lynn Swann took ballet to be a better football player." M. J. spoke directly to Tag.

Mrs. Rooney rolled her eyes. "She had a natural talent. Don't you think she should've stayed with it?"

Tag was trapped in the middle. He looked at Judge Rooney, thinking now would be a good time for the man to level some judicial balance.

"At least it taught her to stand up straighter," the man said. "Remember how she used to slouch?"

"Oh, heavens, yes," Mrs. Rooney said with a laugh.

"Because I was taller than everyone else," M. J. snapped.

He wanted to get up and go, and take her with him.

"Nonsense, you have the most beautiful, long legs. What I wouldn't give to be built like you!" Mrs. Rooney exclaimed. "You're breathtaking, but you won't even wear a dress to show off what you've got. It's such a shame nobody gets to see those legs."

It was a compliment with a bite. If it hurt Tag to hear it, he could only imagine what it did to M. J. This was the most stressful dinner he'd ever had, and that put dinner with his brothers in perspective. He would break bread with Jordon and Grey any day, and he would enjoy every bite from now on.

"I get to see her legs," Tag blurted. "And I'm fine with being the only one who gets to see them."

Mrs. Rooney made a weird sort of gurgle in her throat, while M. J. chuckled.

Judge Rooney cleared his throat. "Do you enjoy your work with the baseball team?" He enunciated every word of the change of subject with the command that came from professional success and impressive education. He set his shiny fork and knife on either side of his snow-white plate and dabbed his lips with an equally pristine cloth napkin before smoothing non-existent wrinkles from his designer golf shirt.

Perfection. There was a time Tag would've admired the restraint, strived for it even. Now, it seemed uptight and uncomfortable.

Tag nodded. "Yes, I do enjoy my work. I didn't expect to end up in sports medicine, but a rotation proved I had a knack for the musculoskeletal system. From there on, I set out to find a place in baseball." The words made him smile, because he'd done it. Like his mother said, he'd proved Francis Kemmons wrong.

"Admirable."

"It must be so exciting to work with professional athletes," Mrs. Rooney said.

If exciting was diagnosing rashes and passing out allergy medicine, because that unfortunately was the norm, which was exactly why working with Grey had mattered so much in the first place. It was also why Tag had talked to Pop the other night about opening a training room in the gym where he could treat more kids like Dante. A change of pace. One that did much more than pad Tag's resume and line his pocketbook.

"It's very satisfying," Tag said, glancing at M. J. who was uncharacteristically quiet. He wanted to draw her into this conversation. "I have great respect for elite athletes. I guess you could say it was drilled into me at an early age." Yeah, that probably wasn't the smartest thing to say, because it caused a burning in his throat, and he reached for his water glass to hide his discomfort.

Judge Rooney nodded, and Mrs. Rooney offered a breathy, "Me, too. Most people don't look at ballet as a sport, but in my heyday, my endurance and muscle tone was second to none."

Tag agreed. "I see a good number of dancers in my practice. Their bodies take a beating."

"It's brutal."

"When it comes to sports, anything worth achieving is, especially at the professional level. It takes a level of commitment many of us don't have the guts to make, which is why I have great pride in and respect for M. J."

She looked up then, first at Tag, and then at her parents. She said nothing, but the lift of her chin conveyed some sort of challenge.

Tag looked at her parents, too. They sat stone-faced. "I'm sure you share my sentiments."

"I do," Judge Rooney finally said. He had the most miserable, condescending delivery. If Tag didn't understand English, he'd have sworn the man said something unpleasant just from the tone of his voice.

M. J. tipped her head, seemingly focusing on her stepmother.

"Doctor Howard …" Mrs. Rooney started.

It probably wasn't worth his breath to ask that she call him Tag again. After all, M. J. hated her given name, and, yet, they refused to respect her wish to be called M. J.

"We love our Maya Jane," she continued. "We just wish she would recognize the fact that age and gender do come into play with things like this, and there does come a time when one should grow up, give up those tomboy ways, and move on to the respectable, responsible things in life. I'm sure a traditional man like you can understand." She had this way of lifting her nose in superiority, and then batting her lashes to smooth over the snobbery.

M.J.'s fork clanged against her plate, and a twisted smile curved her lips. "I should've known nothing could ever really be different. You couldn't accept me unless you succeeded in changing me."

"Maya Jane, don't be so dramatic," Mrs. Rooney said, sighing with exasperation. "I was just giving Dr. Howard some background. You've asked us to make an attempt, and we're making one. You have to give us some time to adjust."

M. J. snorted an exhale. "Fine. You know what? Take as much time as you want, but I'm done."

"Done?" her father repeated, and Tag thought he actually saw some emotion—perhaps even a bit of fear—flash on the man's face. "And what exactly do you mean by—"

"For years. I've been saying that I'm okay with who I am. And I am, but you're not. And there was always that small part of me that wanted your approval. All the texts practically begging you to come to see my games. That's done. From now on, if you want to see me, you're going to have to make one-hundred percent of the effort. If you can't accept me like this, then that's your problem. I'm done trying to make you love me just the way I am."

Her head was high, her eyes blazing with confidence. How could her parents not see how amazing she was? So strong and brave. Tag knew the kind of fortitude it took to stand up to the people you loved—the people who were supposed to love you no matter what—when they said you weren't good enough. If he'd had half her courage as a kid, maybe his life would've been different.

Tag reached out for M. J.'s hand, lacing his fingers with hers, and turned to face Mr. and Mrs. Rooney. "I love M. J. just the way she is. In fact, I love her *because* she is the way she is."

He felt heat from her stare on the right side of his face. It crawled over his cheek until it engulfed his head. He'd said he loved her out loud in a way that really couldn't be misconstrued.

Sweat beaded Tag's brow and he felt the tingle in his palms. His natural instinct was to shrink back, avoid the discomfort, and let go of M. J.'s hand. Instead he took a deep breath and squeezed it tighter.

He wasn't going to run from this relationship.

Chapter Sixteen

M. J. had never been so happy to know Tag lived in the suburbs a short drive away from her parents. She just wanted to be alone with him, to thank him, to talk to him.

As she sat beside him in the car, listening to a radio broadcast of an away baseball game, she went over the evening in her head. He'd kept up conversation with her parents when she couldn't manage to do the same. He'd complimented her football playing … and her legs. She looked out the passenger side window to hide her smile. Of course, he'd done more than compliment her with those words—he'd defended her, too. That felt good. Really good. Almost as good as hearing the L-word on his lips.

I love M. J. just the way she is.

But maybe she was reading too much into it. He hadn't expressed a similar sentiment since. In fact, he was uncharacteristically quiet. Though dinner with her parents could have that effect on people. They'd pretty much shut down after she spoke her mind, leading to a hasty dessert and early exit. It didn't matter. She really was done trying to please them, and Tag had helped her see that it was time to say that.

She looked at him, so handsome, and so much stronger than he knew. Slipping a hand behind his neck, she moved closer until her lips were just below his ear.

"Thank you," she said, placing a kiss on his cologne-scented cheek.

He reached up and cupped her face, holding her there. "For what?"

"For everything you did to keep me from losing my mind."

"Anytime." He turned his head just enough to meet her lips.

When she resettled in her seat, her heart was racing, and it wasn't from the chaste kiss. How long had she known him? She used games played to keep track of the time. The season started in early April. She fell right around then, because she was cleared in time for the home opener. It was May, late May. Seven weeks? Was that enough time to see your future alongside someone else's?

They'd had enough time to develop a friendship and start a physical relationship, to break apart and come back together again. They'd had enough time to know things were easier—better— when they were together. When he was down, she propped him up, and he did the same for her. When they were both up, her life was fuller than it had ever been. That was what partnerships were about—not changing someone to fit a preferred mold, not leaving them behind when they didn't. *Love.*

She squeezed her hands together in her lap. What if she did love him? What happened next? There were little things, technicalities that tripped up relationships all the time. Seemingly compatible couples fought over careers. They separated over things like religions … or kids. She looked out the window again.

She was so far ahead of this game she feared she was about to blow it before the snap, but still, she opened her mouth and the words tumbled out. "Can I ask you something?"

Tag smiled at her, but it was a shaky smile. "I think I know what you're going to ask me."

"You do?" Her face heated.

"Yep, but go ahead."

She took a deep breath. "Do you ever think about having kids?"

His eyebrows rose, like she'd surprised him with the question. Her heartbeat stuttered.

"Sometimes," he said, his brows lowering to a more speculative position. The car slowed as he pulled into his driveway and the garage door lifted. He looked at her with the same considering expression on his face, but it was like he was staring straight through her. "Especially after seeing Jordon's son." He blinked, and his gaze flitted over her face. "After everything I've been through, I think I'd be a good dad."

If he stood up for his kids the way he stood up for her, definitely. "I think you would be, too."

"How about you? Do you want kids?"

He was smiling again, that lopsided grin that drew her to him in the first place, the look that said he somehow knew something enjoyable that she didn't.

"I do. Someday." That day was far, far away, and she was crazy for even bringing this topic up, like it was the crux of a job interview. What was she going to do, grill him about religion next?

She looked straight ahead as he pulled into the garage. "Being with my parents makes me think of those things," she said, hoping to reasonably justify the conversation with something other than love and marriage. Two things she hadn't been sure she'd ever wanted … until Tag.

A mountain bike hung on the back wall alongside golf clubs and a snow shovel. Her palms continued their manic squeezing. This was not the sort of life she imagined. Luxury cars, suburban neighborhoods, and a neat freak. Her version went more like: economy cars, warehouse districts, and a rescue cat who wouldn't mind being left home alone every other weekend.

Tag opened her car door and offered his hand.

Could she be happy here? Was he happy here?

"Do you think you'll always live in the suburbs?" she asked.

His grin was positively lethal, deepening the V-shape of his jaw and sparkling in his eyes. "Miss Rooney, if I didn't know any better I'd think you were entertaining thoughts of settling down with me." The same brows that rose with surprise a moment ago were bobbing with amusement.

She shoved him playfully. There was no use hiding it now. "What if I am?"

"Then that would be excellent." His mouth met hers in a silky brush that tickled her skin and curled her toes. "And to answer your other question: wherever you lead, I will follow."

Her insides melted. "You have no idea the kind of power you are giving me."

"Oh, yes I do." Tag gripped her hand and led her up the stairs.

The light over the stove was on, illuminating their way into the kitchen. It struck M. J. as such a sweet, old-fashioned thing to do. This man without the usual hang-ups about gender roles and expectations was still traditional enough to leave a light on like her grandmother used to do. Simple and sweet. He defied logic, and she loved that about him. She loved all of him.

"I love you," she said, facing him. The words were straight and to the point, and just how she liked her tequila—without a chaser. No stipulations, no restrictions, no suggestion that she would love him more if he could only just change this one little thing.

Tag closed the gap between them, sliding arms around her waist, pressing her body against his, sighing against the sensitive skin at the base of her neck.

"You said it at dinner, and I, well … maybe that was just for my parents' benefit," she said, wanting desperately to project some strength and independence in this moment of incredible vulnerability.

"What if I do, and it wasn't?" he whispered, licking the curve of her ear.

"Then that." she said with a shudder, "would be excellent."

It didn't erase any bumps in the road ahead. After all, she still had a championship to win. But knowing the feeling was mutual sure did make for a magical night.

In fact, she doubted anything could top it.

• • •

Love was a strange sort of thing, one that made Tag send mushy text messages in between patients and hide in Jordon's guest room bath just to have a private conversation with M. J. while he was away. Being apart for a few days was difficult after seeing her almost every day for two weeks, but it was the right thing to do—for both of them. This article and photo shoot were the ultimate show of solidarity with his brothers, and M. J. needed alone time to prepare for the championship game looming over next weekend.

Besides, he'd be back in Cleveland tomorrow.

When Tag finally rejoined the group on the sprawling deck behind Jordon and Maggie's Lake Norman home, he missed M. J. even more. She would've loved this scenery. Beyond the gently sloping, lush, green yard, a couple jet skis carved the shiny water. The sun blazed, turning everything it touched into a sparkling version of itself, including Jordon's new speedboat.

"I don't understand how you can buy a boat like that and never take it out," Grey teased.

"You're more than welcome to take her out. I don't mind sharing." Jordon grinned.

"We are talking about the boat, aren't we?" Grey winced when Maggie backhanded him in the gut from her seated position.

"Hey! I thought you were a pacifist," he complained as he rubbed his stomach—with a damn-near fully operational right hand.

Tag smiled and leaned forward, snagging a grape from the tray in the middle of the table.

"How's M. J.?" Nel asked, never taking her eyes off the sleeping baby in her arms. One of Braydon's chubby legs rested in her palm, and she stroked his skin with her thumb. Every once in a while, Tag caught her stealing a wistful look at Grey. Babies had that effect on people.

"She's good," he said, entertaining a few mental images of M. J. in Nel's place. Only they turned comical when the woman in his head tucked the baby against her side in a classic football hold. "She's practicing hard through the bye week and focusing on the next game. It's the 'biggest game of her mother-freaking career'—a direct quote." He chuckled.

"We'll be there," Nel said, which was reasonable since the game was in Pittsburgh, but it was an incredibly nice gesture all the same.

"Thank you."

Before Tag could add how much it would mean to M. J., Grey elbowed Jordon who was standing alongside him, leaning on the deck railing. "You guys should come in," he said. "Just an overnight trip if that's all you can swing."

"I would like to see her play," Jordon said. "But I have to be in Guatemala the Monday following, which reminds me …" He pointed at Tag. "I need to talk to you about this pitcher I'm going to see. The kid has some genetic malformity. I don't have all the details, but longevity of the arm could be an issue. Anyhow, that's neither here nor there. Maybe I could work it so I was flying out of Pittsburgh straight to Guatemala." He rested his gorilla-like hands on Maggie's lithe shoulders. "What would you say to that?"

She tilted her head until she was looking at him. "I'm flexible."

"Baby, I know you are." He kissed her amid Grey's gagging sounds.

Tag laughed.

"Then it's settled," Nel said. "We are the official M. J. Rooney cheering section. Ooh! And I'll ask my family to come so we're extra loud."

"M. J. will love that," Tag said.

Truth be told, he loved it, too—the support, the camaraderie, the connection. Being a part of the Kemmons family wasn't a curse after all. It filled in the holes of his life and completed him—like M. J. did.

Tag breathed deeply as he settled back in his chair and stared at the postcard-worthy lake scene. The empty chair beside him took on symbolic meaning.

"If they win this game, I'm going to ask her to marry me."

Maggie squealed, waking the baby and scaring the crap out of Tag, whose heart rate was already high.

Nel passed Braydon to Maggie and landed in the empty seat beside Tag. "I love this idea. Did you buy the ring?"

Tag roughed a hand over his face. "No. I just thought of it actually."

"It's so romantic," Maggie cooed. "How do you think you'll do it?"

"He doesn't know. He just thought of it," Jordon said, chuckling. "Sorry, man, but now you're stuck, because these two will hound you until you do it."

Tag managed a weak smile. "I have no idea how I'm going to do it. I'm open to suggestions."

"Babe, help the man," Nel said, her eyes sparkling at the man who walked up behind her. "Grey is the master of romantic gestures."

"Master …" Jordon mused. "Does that mean he uses whips and chains?"

"Hush," Maggie said.

"You know what I mean, Jordon," Nel shot him a pointed look and then turned her attention back to Tag, laying a hand on his forearm. "Grey proposed on the day that we met with the real estate attorney to add me to the deed of the house. After everything was final, he placed a ring of keys in my hand, and told me the decorative keychain was special, and it was … really elaborate, all sparkly and colorful, and hanging in the very middle was this." She flashed her left hand at Tag, showing off an impressive diamond. "And then …" She gripped his arm, "he said, 'You have my heart. You have my home. Now, have my ring.'"

Maggie sighed.

Nel smiled as she wiped a tear from her eye and reached behind her to grab hold of Grey's hand.

"Sap," Jordon teased.

Tag nodded. "I don't know if I can pull off something that smooth."

"Bro, it's easy," Grey said, puffing out his chest a bit. "You give the ring to the referee and have him hand it to her at the coin toss."

"And then she loses the game because she's in emotional shock. Nice," Jordon said.

A heavy ball of nerves settled in Tag's stomach, but his heart thudded a normal beat. "Agreed. And keep in mind, she could always say no."

Nel gasped. "Why would she do that?"

"We haven't been together that long. Don't you think it's a little soon?"

Conspiratorial glances tossed around the table.

"Dude, you are asking the wrong bunch that question," Grey said.

"Do you love her?" Maggie asked.

Grey and Jordon groaned.

"Are we going to need a couch for this?" Grey asked. "Or can he just lie down on the deck?"

"Smart ass," Maggie said, but she was smiling. "Answer the question, Tag."

"Yes, I love her."

Maggie opened her mouth, but Jordon beat her to the next question. "Does she love you?" He smiled at his wife. "See, I'm learning from watching you." She smacked a quick kiss to his lips, cradling their child between them.

Tag wanted a moment like that with M. J. more than he wanted his next breath.

"Does she?" Nel asked, repeating Jordon's question.

"She does," Tag said, remembering her beautiful face when she blurted the words in his kitchen. At the memory alone his body swelled with so much joy he thought he might explode.

"Then she's not going to say no," Nel said.

Heads nodded around the table, making the sentiment unanimous.

"So, bro … go big or go home," Grey said.

"At least let her finish the game," Jordon added.

"That could work!" Nel sat up so fast the back of her chair shook. "What if you proposed after the game?"

Tag imagined himself standing outside the locker room door with a ring in hand. It seemed cheesy somehow. Probably because in his mind he was flanked by his family, which was appropriate, considering they were active participants in the planning.

He smiled at the crew around the table, waiting for his response. "Okay." He put up his hands to halt the cheers. "*If* she wins, I'll propose after the game. I'll have the ring with me, and I'll figure out how I'm going to do it and what I'm going to say between now and then, but if they lose, I'm going to wait for a happier day, so you'll have to be prepared to keep quiet a little longer."

And he'd have to be prepared to be a nervous wreck until the day she said yes.

Chapter Seventeen

M. J. pushed in her earphone buds and settled her head in the crook between her seat back and the bus window. She didn't feel like talking. Championship pursuits were a great conversation killer.

The classic rock music drowned out thought—most of it. As she stared at the edge of the parking lot where the asphalt met the trees, X's and O's aligned in playbook formation. It was no surprise. She saw this stuff in her sleep. With any luck, that was exactly what would be happening for the next two hours while the bus made its way to Pittsburgh. Then she'd wake up ready for team and media meetings.

A bony object dug into her shoulder, and she turned to see Tanya, waving a piece of paper in one hand and gesturing for M. J. to take her earphones out with the other.

"Yeah?" M. J. asked, pulling one bud from her ear.

"Can you get Doc to sign this?"

M. J. took the rolled piece of paper fluttering in front of her face and locked eyes with a gorgeous Tag, stethoscope hanging loosely around the neckline of his white coat. Beside him on the right, stood Grey in full uniform, leaning on the end of a baseball bat. On the other side of Tag stood Jordon decked out in an impressive business suit. Neither one of the men smiled. The crisp, white background made them leap off the page, along with the title in rich, red, block letters: *The Kemmons Connection: How One Family Is Taking Major League Baseball by Storm.*

The breath caught in her throat, forcing her to press her lips together so she didn't make some embarrassing sound.

"Kinda cool, huh?" Tanya sat in the empty seat beside M. J.

The bus jerked to start, and still M. J. stared at the piece of printer paper in her hand. "It's not due on stands for a few days. Where'd you get this?"

"Online. I was messing around in the gym office before I headed over here. They had it up as a subscription teaser. Didn't you get a sneak peak from Doc?"

M. J. shook her head. He'd been giving her plenty of space, letting her control things, including conversation. He said he understood the mind of an athlete, and she'd thanked him with a wild night in bed. Now she was sad she'd missed an early glimpse of this. *This* was epic.

"I can't wait to read the article," she said. He'd told her enough about the experience for her to know it went well—directly opposite from the radio interview. "I'll ask him to sign this, but don't you want to wait for the actual issue?"

"Oh, believe me, I will. I'm going to sell that one." She leaned into M. J. with a laugh. "Actually, I'm going to give this one to Dad, so he can hang it in his office."

M. J. nodded, feeling the tingle of tears behind her eyes. Tag had been working with Pop to establish a sports medicine clinic inside the gym. To see him take a genuine interest in the people and places she loved only solidified her belief they were meant to be together.

"Okay, I'll leave you alone so you can *prepare*." Tanya wiggled her fingers in the air all goofball-mystical as she stood.

M. J. smiled and settled against the window again, glancing at the printout on her lap. She should put it away, go back to daydreaming about X's and O's of the football variety—not the other kind. But, man, did she like life with a healthy dose of both.

Looking at the picture again, she permitted herself a small sigh of approval before she stuffed her earphone buds back in place. She'd give it until the Ohio-Pennsylvania border before she rolled it up and put it away.

The next day was game day. Tag had called during breakfast to say he was headed for Pittsburgh. He ended the call with a "good luck" and an "I love you." In all the games she'd played, she couldn't remember a smaller collection of words having such a spirit-boosting effect. She was pretty sure she could walk on water by the time the team bus reached the field.

Too bad the playing field was made of hot, hard turf. M. J. hurt after being driven into it by any number of Mack trucks—over and over again. Halfway through the first quarter, she pleaded with her O-line in the huddle, "I can't take much more of this."

Third and eighteen on the heels of false start and holding calls, M. J. settled under center and dropped back for a post route pass. On her sixth step, one before her release, something hard and relentless drove into her left flank followed by a helmet-to-helmet blow that rattled her brain and rang in her ears. She crumpled to the turf, taking the brunt of the fall on her right shoulder.

Fuck. Everything burned.

M. J. opened her eyes when she heard Dr. Ridge say her name. *Focus.* If she couldn't answer his questions coherently, she'd be pulled.

"What hurts?"

"Shoulder," she said, even though it was a drop in the pain bucket compared to the searing in her jaw and neck. The closer any of her aches got to the head, the more likely they'd be to suspect a concussion. Maybe they already did. She had no idea if she passed out after that hit.

They poked and prodded her shoulder, helping her into a sitting position, removing her helmet. She fought the urge to close her eyes and curl up on the ground.

"We're going to observe her for a series or two," Dr. Ridge said.

M. J. didn't like any downtime in a game this big, but she knew the rules and regulations couldn't be argued with. Her best bet was to cling to normalcy on the sidelines and insist they put her back in to start the second quarter.

Revis on one side, Dr. Ridge on the other, they helped her off the field. Her goal was to walk a straight and strong line with head up and eyes wide and focused.

Her teammates rode the sideline, concern on their faces. M. J. looked away from them to the cheering crowd. She saw Tag first, standing alone in the center aisle against the front railing. If she thought her teammates looked concerned, Tag looked downright terrified. He pointed to his head. She shook hers slightly, mindful that balance would be an issue with a true concussion, and she didn't want to wind up back on her ass.

He dropped his chin and gave her a pointed look that said, "You better not be lying to me."

She forced a smile, because she didn't need him hopping the railing and coming down on the field. This was supposed to be her big game, her big day. She wasn't going to let a little headache stand in the way.

M. J. was about to take a seat on the bench when something fluttered beside Tag in her peripheral vision. It was Nel, waving like crazy and then giving two thumbs up. Beside Nel was Grey, and then came Maggie with Braydon in a carrier on her chest, and Jordon, too. Behind them was Edna Dean. And what she saw next packed a bigger punch than any outside linebacker ever could. Dad's face appeared over Jordon's shoulder. Felicia was there, too. At an away game. It was the kind of undeniable support M. J. had only ever dreamed about.

A blast of emotion numbed her face and dried her wide eyes. She finally had her own personal cheering section big enough to rival Tanya's.

Turning around without a worry for her head and keeping her balance the entire time, M. J. called out to Coach, "Put me in."

"Rooney, sit," he said with his eyes on the field.

She walked to him. "Put me in." The harsh whisper scraped her throat.

And when he did, she was determined not to let anyone down.

This was going to be a day none of them would forget.

•••

"She shouldn't be back in after a hit like that. This is crazy." Tag resisted Nel's tugs on his arm in the direction of his seat and gave a death stare in Dave Ridge's direction. "I hold you personally responsible," Tag yelled.

Dave shrugged, like he had no control over the woman. Under different circumstances, Tag would've vouched for that. But a team physician had to suspect an elite athlete in the biggest game of her career would lie like a rug to get back into the game.

"Down in front," someone yelled.

"Relax," Nel added, tugging him again.

Fine. Tag sat, but he didn't relax, and he didn't take his eyes off M. J. "If she gets hit again or she looks off, I'm going down there."

"She'll be okay," Grey said, leaning across Nel and smacking Tag's knee. "I face-planted on the outfield wall in Pittsburgh and played the whole game with a concussion, and nothing bad happened to me."

"Arguable, babe." Nel's chuckle did nothing to lift Tag's spirits.

He leaned forward, studying M. J. as she dropped back to pass and released a short spiral for a completion and an eleven-yard gain. She looked okay. When she dropped back and handed off, she looked good, too. But she brought Tag to his feet when she kept the ball and scrambled for a fifteen-yard gain, ducking out of bounds seconds before what could've been one hell of a collision.

"Sit," Mom said, swatting him on the ass. "She doesn't need to look up here and see you worrying."

"I'm doing enough of that for all of us," Mrs. Rooney shouted. Her investment in the game was even more shocking than her presence. Tag only wished he could settle down enough to enjoy her enthusiasm.

Halftime came and went with the Clash down by fourteen.

When Dave trotted to the sideline before the team returned from the locker room, Tag leaned over the railing to ask, "How is she?"

"Mad," Dave said, laughing. "Have you seen the score?"

"I'm talking about her head."

"If the eloquent, vulgarity-filled tirade she just had in the locker room is any indication of her mental condition, she's doing great."

Somehow, that put Tag at ease. Now, a couple touchdowns, a field goal and the end of the game would have him downright euphoric. He patted the ring box in his right pants pocket.

He'd assembled all these people for more than a football game.

The first sign of life from the Clash defense in the second half came from a fumble recovery returned for a touchdown. A thirty-two-yard field goal quickly followed. M. J. finally seemed to be getting the time in the pocket she needed to execute plays—and stay on her feet. Tag was finding it difficult to stay off his, which was funny, because football had never been his game. Other than caring for the injured athletes, he could take or leave the basic barbarism. But when M. J. played, it was frigging poetry.

"I almost stayed out by the snack bar," Maggie said as she returned to her seat after changing Braydon. "This is too violent and stressful for me."

Tag tweaked his nephew's nose as they passed. "This is where it gets good," he said to Maggie.

His positive words belied the churning in his stomach. This was also were it got serious. With five minutes left, there was enough time for the Clash to score, but there was also plenty of time for Pittsburgh to return the favor.

Clock management would be key. He'd seen M. J. play enough to know she was capable of controlling the pace of this game. He had faith in her—even when she threw an interception in the middle of an impressive forty-yard drive.

"Crap," Nel said.

Tag cringed at that tone of resignation in her voice.

"There's lots of time," Grey added.

And Tag tossed an appreciative nod to him. If they lost, there would be more football games next year, and he would still find another way, another day to propose. But a win, and this—he patted the ring box again—today, in front of their families, would be perfect.

Sometimes striving for perfection was okay.

Again, the Clash defense stepped up, denying Pittsburgh the touchdown on fourth and inches, and softening the blow of the interception, but the clock flashed abysmally low digits.

With under a minute left, Tag tucked the ring deeper into his pocket, acknowledging they'd reached longshot territory. But then a spark of denial balked at his lack of faith and insisted he correct it by pulling out the box and taking a good long look.

The emerald-cut diamond set in platinum glistened in the sun.

"You're going to get to do it," Nel said, looping her arm through his. "Keep your eye on the prize, just like M. J.'s doing."

The plays were hurried but accurate and effective with the wide receivers rushing out of bounds to stop the clock. An unproductive run play and an incomplete pass left time for one more attempt to score. The raucous crowd jumped to its feet, and finally Tag could stand without chastisement.

The snap … the drop … the pass.

The ball floated through the air in slow motion, eventually dropping into the center of a mass of players huddled in the end zone, all reaching for the same thing. M. J.'s usual target got a gloved hand on the ball, but a defender knocked it away.

Tag's breathing stopped.

Again in slow motion, the ball drifted, this time toward the ground. The season, the proposal, all of it poised to shatter … until another Clash receiver dove out, snatching the ball from midair before it hit the ground.

Touchdown. Game over. Clash win.

• • •

M. J. had been dog-piled before, but never after a championship win. As her teammates helped her off the turf, leftover adrenaline buzzed through her veins, making her feel like she was gliding toward the sidelines.

Tanya and Mertz ran up ahead, grabbing the orange jug of water and dumping it over Coach's head. Pure chaos—on the field and in the stands. M. J. looked up and made eye contact with a grinning Tag, hands in his pockets, belly pressed to the railing, looking like he wanted to leap to the ground. She smiled back at him—at all of them. It was still so damn hard to believe they were here.

The team created a sort of tide around her, moving her toward the locker room, where there was cheap champagne and hot showers to be had. As soon as the adrenaline faded, her aching body would be in serious need of that last one. Any other time, she might even linger under the soothing spray, but not today. There would be people waiting for her outside the locker room. A lot of people.

Come to think of it, the adrenaline might never fade. M. J. beamed. This day couldn't possibly get better.

"Rooney." She snapped her head in the direction of Coach's booming voice. He dabbed his wet head with a towel. "Somebody's looking for you on the field."

Hopefully a reporter. It was about time this team got the recognition it deserved.

M. J. turned around, bobbing her head for a better look as she made her way back up the ramp. The crowd of players before her parted, and through it walked Tag. His grin was wobbly. His eyes were wide. And something about the expression on his gorgeous face told her this wasn't about saying a simple "good game."

The adrenaline surged, causing her to splay a hand across her chest to keep her heart from jumping out of her skin.

Tag dropped to one knee.

Her teammates cheered.

"M. J. Rooney with a rocket for an arm," his grin widened, "I love you."

Between the noises all around her and the pounding of her heart echoing in her ears, she could barely hear him, but she could read those beautiful lips, and she knew exactly what that fairytale posture meant.

He held out a hand, reaching for her, and she felt a push from behind. In a flash, she was grabbing onto him.

"Will you marry me?" He presented a brilliant ring in a little black box.

M. J. laughed when a few of her teammates hollered, "Yes!"

And then she dropped to her knees before him, wanting more than anything to make this moment last, to emblazon it on her brain so she'd never forget a detail of his beautiful, joyful face.

"You look good on my field," she said.

"You look better."

When he smiled, an overwhelming feeling of déjà vu made M. J. woozy. They'd been like this before on a field. When she fell. It was like her heart had always remembered, even when her head couldn't.

"Answer him," someone yelled.

That was the right thing to do. She could ogle him later. In fact, for the rest of their lives if she wanted to.

She leaned in, inches from his mouth, making it as intimate as possible. "Yes, I'll marry you."

The crowd cheered, but for once, she didn't care about their accolades or approval.

Now and forever more, the only fan she needed was him.

The End

About the Author

Elley Arden is a born and bred Pennsylvanian who has lived as far west as Utah and as far north as Wisconsin. She drinks wine like it's water (a slight exaggeration), prefers a night at the ball-park to a night on the town, and believes almond English toffee is the key to happiness. Elley writes contemporary romances for Crimson Romance. For a complete list of Elley's books, visit *www. elleyarden.com.*

More from This Author
(From *Change My Mind* by Elley Arden)

Nel slammed the brakes and strangled the steering wheel, fighting the urge to close her eyes, praying at least one dog cleared her Volvo's front end. Miraculously, both animals escaped disaster, dodging her car and scrambling across the empty lanes of traffic. They disappeared behind the big red sign that still made Nel's heart skip a beat more than a year after its first appearance.

Parker Properties, Inc.—as in Penelope Parker. The satisfaction of owning a real estate agency never faded.

Smoothing her right hand beneath the navy blue lapel of her wool suit coat, Nel welcomed the vibration of her heart against her hand. Of course, this bout of breathlessness was more than likely related to the kamikaze dogs ... a skinny Rottweiler and a mangy golden retriever who were now eye-deep in the office's trash.

Apparently the mess-maker of the last couple weeks wasn't a raccoon.

Parking in her usual spot to the right of the front door, Nel left her briefcase and Monday's bag of bagels on the passenger seat to launch from the car with three sharp claps.

"Get outta there!" she yelled, second-guessing the brazen scare tactic when her voice hit the ice-cold air.

First the golden turned lackluster eyes on her, then the rottie. They looked sad, sick, and painfully thin. Their ribs lined the sparse fur of their bellies, and their tails hung between their legs.

"Poor babies." Nel exhaled, careful not to make any sudden movements. Hungry dogs could become mean dogs in the blink of an eye, something she should've thought about before she brought their full, agitated attention on her.

Fortunately there was no attempt to run her off, no growling or lips curling. Instead, a pitiful, phantom whine arose from one of the dogs as they both returned their noses to the garbage pile. Too bad there wasn't much edible in the black bags—a few pieces of crust from Friday's impromptu pizza lunch if they were lucky, certainly not enough to satisfy two starving dogs.

Nel turned back to the car, leaned across the front seat, and snagged the bag of bagels. Removing the carton of cream cheese, napkins, and plastic knives, she ripped a bagel in three pieces and tossed the chunks toward the animals, who jerked when the bagels thumped against the pavement.

They spied her, widening their stances, a type of standoff between foes. When Nel was sure her efforts were futile, the golden moved closer, nose to the ground, as if the bagel could be sucked through his flaring nostrils.

"Thatta girl," Nel whispered, having no idea whether or not the endearment fit. She tilted her head, looking for signs of manhood, only to roll her eyes at the awkward search.

And then the rottie moved. Five seconds later, the bagel pieces were devoured, and Nel had two new friends—friends who were desperate for more food, some water, and a good hot bath.

"What the heck is going on out here?" Rena poked her rounded face and large green eyes around the front door. "That better not be my asiago."

Nel looked at the last piece of asiago bagel in her hand and then back to Rena. "I'll buy you more."

The dogs bolted for the open door, dashing past Rena and into the office.

"Are you kidding me?" Rena yelled. "Get them out."

"They're cold." Nel picked up her pace and reached for the door, holding it open as they followed the dogs inside.

"They can't be here."

"They're strays."

The rottie tipped over a small trash can with his tail while the golden stuck her nose into an open filing cabinet.

Rena groaned. "They can't stay."

"Of course they can't stay, but I can't let them loose to get hit by a car. Come here, guys." Nel hunched over and patted palms to her knees.

To her surprise, the dogs obeyed. And as she smoothed hands over their course fur, she noticed collars and tags.

"Can you get a look at their tags?" Nel asked, holding the dogs' attention with soft, steady strokes to their bony heads.

"They're dirty, they smell; I'm sure they have fleas. I'm not touching them."

"Rena, I'm not asking you to hug them. Just bend over and peek at the tags." Some days Nel regretted hiring her best friend. The familiarity led to more than a few moments of dissonance. But hiring Rena was sort of a mercy mission. Nobody aspired to be thirty, working part-time at a pretzel stand in the mall. And Nel couldn't let Rena think that was all she was good for.

Rena rattled off a telephone number. "Remember 5293," she said, scrambling to her desk, digging through her top drawer. "Damn it! I need more pens."

"Do you eat them?" Nel teased, still rubbing the tired-looking dogs behind the ears.

"Funny. What was the number I told you to remember?"

"5293." Nel looked around the reception area. "Do we have something I can use to give them water?"

"The bucket the cleaners use for mopping," Rena said, holding the desk phone to her ear.

"I'm not going to let them drink out of something with chemical residue."

"They were eating out of the garbage. I hardly think it matters."

It mattered. They didn't deserve to be subjected to more harm. By the looks of them, they'd been through so much already. Nel stared into their sad eyes and smiled while she made a mental tour of the office, settling on a plastic bowl full of blank nametags in the supply closet.

"No answer, and the mailbox is full. Now what?" Rena perched on the edge of her desk.

"Get me the plastic bowl from the supply closet filled with water, and then we'll think of something."

Nel hated to call the shelter … actually, she refused. There were plenty of rescues around town who would ensure the dogs were rehabbed and given good homes. Before she reached out to one of them, she would do whatever she could to find the animals' owner.

The rottie slumped to the hardwood floor, leaving Nel petting the golden. With a tiny movement, Nel moved her hand lower on the golden's neck, combing her nails through the fur, inching closer to the buckle. If she could just get a good look at the tags …

"Where do you want it?" Rena walked toward them with the bowl.

"Right here." Nel gestured to the floor at her feet and stepped back while unlatching the collar in one fluid movement. She glanced at the tags in her hand. "The golden's name is Blackjack." The telephone number Rena called was etched below the name. Beneath that tag nestled a county-issued tag. "I wonder if they can trace the dogs by this number."

It was worth a phone call.

While the dogs drank, Nel made the call, and sure enough, the ID number on Blackjack's tag led to the address used to license the dog—an address that wasn't far away. Nel glanced at the dogs, resting on the drenched floor, noses centimeters from the water bowl, and satisfaction squared her shoulders. She was going to get these boys home, and home was … she Googled the address, nearly dropping the phone when she looked at the satellite map.

"Oh. My. God." She pointed to her cell phone screen. "Rena, these dogs belong at Castle Chaos."

Castle Chaos was the single greatest piece of residential architecture in the South Hills. The kind of property that could put a small, struggling real estate agency on the radar of every other agency in Pittsburgh.

"I suppose that's fitting," Rena sneered. "Decrepit animals belong in a decrepit house."

Nel waved off the cynicism. "That house is worth millions."

"To a vampire in Transylvania."

"I love that house."

"You also love slasher movies. Your taste is questionable."

Nel stuck out her tongue rather than defend her cinematic choices once again. "I'm going to drive the dogs over there."

"In your car?"

"No, in yours." She cast Rena a sarcastic grin and clapped to get the dogs' attention.

Everything happened for a reason. These dogs, coming from that house, now being in her office, had *business opportunity* written all over it. Maybe the old, rich guy who owned the place would be so thankful to see his dogs returned safely, he'd admit he couldn't keep up with the house anymore, and he'd agree to let Nel be the listing agent. She smiled as she slid behind the wheel of her car with the dogs safely in the backseat.

One of these days, Nel Parker was going to look back on this moment and remember it as the moment when everything changed.

•••

Elevator music on the other end of the cell phone threatened to drive Grey insane. If his teeth weren't being ground to bits out of frustration, they'd be chattering, shaking along with the rest of his chilled body. *How hard was it to get a boiler fixed in the dead of winter?*

"We can have the technician there tomorrow morning, tomorrow afternoon at the latest."

Apparently pretty damn hard.

"That's the best you can do?" Grey growled.

"I'm afraid so, sir. Looking at past maintenance records I can tell you … that particular boiler is a special case."

Of course it was, because Grey's father never did anything reasonable.

With a grunt of concession he ended the call, sliding the cell phone across the marble counter, careful not to touch the ice-cold stone and add to his misery. He knew returning this house to some semblance of glory was going to be backbreaking work, but he never expected to freeze to death before he drove a single nail.

Scrubbing his palms together, Grey tried to generate some heat; thankful for the beard he left growing long after the Argonauts were eliminated from the postseason. Anonymity was the initial reason for the thick black facial hair, but now there was a practical purpose for not packing a razor or shaving cream. He needed warmth, but he needed more than the beard and the six-burner gas stove were supplying.

A limestone fireplace loomed over the great room, offering an easy solution now that the boiler wasn't going to be fixed until tomorrow. Grey didn't like the idea of using a fireplace that hadn't been serviced in God-only-knew how long, but he'd have to take his chances.

First things first. He grabbed a yellowed, brittle newspaper off the pile he had collected from the front stoop. With a twist, the paper turned into a makeshift torch, and he lit it with the blue gas flame. After turning off the stove, he carried the burning paper into the great room, where he ducked his head beneath the massive limestone blocks and reached an arm into the flue. He hoped the draft would carry the smoke from the paper up the chimney, and out of the house. *That* was the sign he was waiting for as he hunched over, holding his breath.

For once, since he arrived at this empty, sorry house, something miraculously went his way. The smoke curled in ribbons up the chimney and Grey dropped the newspaper to the firebox floor. Now, all he needed was some wood; and from the looks of the overgrown grounds surrounding the house, he wouldn't have a problem finding it.

Making his way through the cavernous, sparsely decorated icebox, he made another trip to the basement; this time ignoring the mammoth boiler and heading for the dingy workroom, where he noticed an axe propped against the cement block wall. Trudging back up the stairs and through the house with axe in tow, his anger grew until the combination of movement and emotion had him breaking into a sweat. *Fuck you, Dad,* he thought for about the millionth time since the bastard ran off to Bermuda—taking Grey's longtime girlfriend along for the ride.

He gripped the axe so hard his knuckles screamed with pain, and for a moment he thought about taking a swing at the ornate trim lining the backdoor. Fortunately for his already-lengthy to-do list, the axe stayed at his side, and his anger peaked. It didn't pass so much as it returned to whatever dark hole Grey stashed it in; leaving him with labored breath and a clenched jaw.

At least he wasn't cold anymore.

Outside in the wind, he made his way through a crunching layer of frozen grass and leaves, to the back of the property where an empty dog run formed a visible boundary between this property and the sloping hillside beyond. He didn't know what happened to the dogs. The lawyer for the estate made no mention of them, so Grey figured his dad had given them away. Then again, maybe he took them to Bermuda. Maybe they were on the plane when it went down—just like Dad and Lindsay.

Grey flinched. He cared more about losing those dogs than he did about losing his father and the woman he had expected to someday marry. With both hands wrapped around the grip of the axe, Grey swung hard at one of the brittle tree trunks littering the frozen ground, feeling the burn in his shoulder and the vibration clear up to his elbows. He stood there, axe lodged in wood, wondering how he got from centerfield in Nashville's brand-new ballpark, to the backyard of a house he didn't want to own. And once again, he was reminded of how his father fucked up everyone's lives.

Yeah? Well, this was where the chain stopped.

Swinging the axe again, noticing less of a protest from his body, Grey reminded himself the house was key to repairing some of the damage his father had caused. All he had to do was fix it up and sell it off, for as close to a million dollars as possible. He swung the axe again, praying to God he could manage the miracle before he needed to report for spring training in a little more than two months. *Two months.* He squeezed his eyes shut as he swung the axe again.

He was crazy. Anyone who discovered what he was doing would agree. This wasn't a job for one man, and yet Grey couldn't figure out how to let anyone else in; how to trust them enough to relinquish the tiniest bit of control. There was too much at stake. He needed to limit the amount of money spent on the renovations, maximize the return on his investment, and sweat out the anger he felt toward his father—and the guilt he felt for not being man enough to stand up to him.

Maybe the daunting task was some sort of self-imposed punishment. After what Grey had done, turning his back on his brother's professional advice and personal support in order to maintain a half-assed relationship with the world's worst dad? This wasn't nearly as harsh of a punishment as he deserved.

Two shrill barks ripped through the frosty silence, and before Grey could turn around he was hit from behind.

"Holy shit." He dropped the axe to rough the dogs behind the ears. "Where'd you come from?"

"They were in my garbage."

She couldn't have been more than five feet tall, standing at the top of the cement walk that led from the front of the house to the back patio. She was dwarfed by the iron gazebo trellises to her left, but there was something formidable about her. Maybe it was the fact that she stood strong despite being sorely underdressed for the current weather conditions. Dressed in nothing but a navy blue pantsuit with her blonde curls whipping around her wind-reddened, heart-shaped face, she was the last sort of thing he expected to see in his father's backyard.

Grey opened his mouth to speak or breathe, but the cold air tightened his throat and chest.

The dogs ran back to her.

"I'm sorry. They belong here, don't they? The county gave me the address based on their license numbers." She bent forward, wrapping each hand around a dog's neck. She looked even smaller in their presence.

Grey blinked, swallowed, and nodded his head; hoping to generate some meaningful thoughts and words to counteract the surprise of seeing the dogs and her … whoever she was. "They belong here."

"Good." She smiled. "I'm sure they're happy to be home. It looks like they've been lost for a while." She patted their thin sides, and anger pinched in his chest. Once again his father's propensity for living a disposable life had hurt more than him.

"Yeah, I … " Grey walked toward her, not knowing what to say exactly, but not wanting to seem rude after she brought the dogs home. He stopped, wondering how close was too close; close enough to be recognized. "I don't know how long they've been gone. I just got here myself."

"Oh." She looked disappointed. Her forehead crinkled and her eyebrows bunched. But when she wound her arms around her body, he figured the cold had finally caught up with her. "You don't live here?"

"No." He was uncomfortable with questions, so he clapped his hands and gestured for the dogs, hoping without them, she'd feel inclined to leave.

"I'm sorry to bother you. Is the homeowner inside? I can knock and let him know I've returned the dogs."

"I'll take it from here." Maybe she was sincere, but it felt like she was digging. Then again, Grey suspected everyone of having an ulterior motive. He'd never been proven wrong. Dressed in a suit like that, she was either an overly nosey neighbor on her lunch break or someone with a business interest in the estate.

Grey didn't want to deal with either.

She hesitated, tightening her arms around her chest, looking over her shoulder at the house, and then back at him. "Are they renovating?"

Clear blue eyes widened and the corner of her lips hitched, like his answer was something she highly anticipated. If he weren't such a miserable bastard, he would've smiled at her enthusiasm—if only because she was so damn pretty.

"I parked behind the dumpster," she continued. "Dumpsters usually signify a reno." She pushed a clump of golden curls off her face and treated him to a blinding smile. "My name's Nel Parker. You may have heard of me or my agency, Parker Properties. I'm a real estate agent, and houses are my passion. I'd love to see what's going on inside … I've admired this property for years."

Yeah, she was pretty, but she was pushy, too.

Grey watched the dogs tear up the hill to the dog run. "Maybe another time. I need to get them taken care of."

"Oh. Of course, I'll just leave you with my card, and you can have the owner get in touch with me at his convenience."

Don't hold your breath, Grey thought as he extended an arm and accepted her card in his hand. Her fingernails brushed the skin he could've sworn was frozen and beyond capable of feeling anything but the pain of frostbite. Instead, the light touch thawed him, and he wrapped warm fingers around the card, squeezing until the card creased; feeling unnerved by his reaction to a perfect stranger.

"Have a good day." She looked around him up the hill to the romping dogs. "Be good boys; stay put." She laughed at herself, and a gust of icy wind lifted her hair, tossing it forward, framing her face like a golden headdress.

Damn. Grey watched her turn and walk away. With her shoulders back, hips swinging and hair whipping out of control, she was like nothing he'd ever seen. Too pretty and too tiny to be taken seriously, and yet he had the feeling she wasn't someone to mess with.

So why was the idea of messing with her so appealing?